# TRUTH OR DARE
## DI SALLY PARKER
### BOOK EIGHT

## M A COMLEY

Copyright © 2022 by M A Comley

All rights reserved.

No part of this book may be reproduced in any form or by any electronic or mechanical means, including information storage and retrieval systems, without written permission from the author, except for the use of brief quotations in a book review.

# ACKNOWLEDGMENTS

Special thanks as always go to @studioenp for their superb cover design expertise.

My heartfelt thanks go to my wonderful editor Emmy, and my proofreaders Joseph and Barbara for spotting all the lingering nits.

Thank you also to my amazing ARC Group who help to keep me sane during this process.

To Mary, gone, but never forgotten. I hope you found the peace you were searching for my dear friend. I miss you each and every day.

## ALSO BY M A COMLEY

Blind Justice (Novella)
Cruel Justice (Book #1)
Mortal Justice (Novella)
Impeding Justice (Book #2)
Final Justice (Book #3)
Foul Justice (Book #4)
Guaranteed Justice (Book #5)
Ultimate Justice (Book #6)
Virtual Justice (Book #7)
Hostile Justice (Book #8)
Tortured Justice (Book #9)
Rough Justice (Book #10)
Dubious Justice (Book #11)
Calculated Justice (Book #12)
Twisted Justice (Book #13)
Justice at Christmas (Short Story)
Prime Justice (Book #14)
Heroic Justice (Book #15)
Shameful Justice (Book #16)
Immoral Justice (Book #17)
Toxic Justice (Book #18)
Overdue Justice (Book #19)
Unfair Justice (a 10,000 word short story)
Irrational Justice (a 10,000 word short story)

Seeking Justice (a 15,000 word novella)
Caring For Justice (a 24,000 word novella)
Savage Justice ( a 17,000 word novella)
Justice at Christmas #2 (a 15,000 word novella)
Gone in Seconds (Justice Again series #1)
Ultimate Dilemma (Justice Again series #2)
Shot of Silence (Justice Again series #3)
Taste of Fury (Justice Again series #4)
Crying Shame (Justice Again series #5)
To Die For (DI Sam Cobbs #1)
To Silence Them (DI Sam Cobbs #2)
To Make Them Pay (DI Sam Cobbs #3)
To Prove Fatal (DI Sam Cobbs #4)
To Condemn Them (DI Sam Cobbs #5)
To Punish Them (DI Sam Cobbs #6)
To Entice Them (DI Sam Cobbs #7)
To Control Them (DI Sam Cobbs #8)
Forever Watching You (DI Miranda Carr thriller)
Wrong Place (DI Sally Parker thriller #1)
No Hiding Place (DI Sally Parker thriller #2)
Cold Case (DI Sally Parker thriller#3)
Deadly Encounter (DI Sally Parker thriller #4)
Lost Innocence (DI Sally Parker thriller #5)
Goodbye My Precious Child (DI Sally Parker #6)
The Missing Wife (DI Sally Parker #7)
Truth or Dare (DI Sally Parker #8)
Web of Deceit (DI Sally Parker Novella with Tara Lyons)
The Missing Children (DI Kayli Bright #1)

Killer On The Run (DI Kayli Bright #2)
Hidden Agenda (DI Kayli Bright #3)
Murderous Betrayal (Kayli Bright #4)
Dying Breath (Kayli Bright #5)
Taken (DI Kayli Bright #6)
The Hostage Takers (DI Kayli Bright Novella)
No Right to Kill (DI Sara Ramsey #1)
Killer Blow (DI Sara Ramsey #2)
The Dead Can't Speak (DI Sara Ramsey #3)
Deluded (DI Sara Ramsey #4)
The Murder Pact (DI Sara Ramsey #5)
Twisted Revenge (DI Sara Ramsey #6)
The Lies She Told (DI Sara Ramsey #7)
For The Love Of… (DI Sara Ramsey #8)
Run for Your Life (DI Sara Ramsey #9)
Cold Mercy (DI Sara Ramsey #10)
Sign of Evil (DI Sara Ramsey #11)
Indefensible (DI Sara Ramsey #12)
Locked Away (DI Sara Ramsey #13)
I Can See You (DI Sara Ramsey #14)
The Kill List (DI Sara Ramsey #15)
Crossing The Line (DI Sara Ramsey #16)
Time to Kill (DI Sara Ramsey #17)
Deadly Passion (DI Sara Ramsey #18)
I Know The Truth (A Psychological thriller)
She's Gone (A psychological thriller)
Shattered Lives (A psychological thriller)
Evil In Disguise – a novel based on True events

Deadly Act (Hero series novella)

Torn Apart (Hero series #1)

End Result (Hero series #2)

In Plain Sight (Hero Series #3)

Double Jeopardy (Hero Series #4)

Criminal Actions (Hero Series #5)

Regrets Mean Nothing (Hero series #6)

Prowlers (Di Hero Series #7)

Sole Intention (Intention series #1)

Grave Intention (Intention series #2)

Devious Intention (Intention #3)

Cozy mysteries

Murder at the Wedding

Murder at the Hotel

Murder by the Sea

Death on the Coast

Death By Association

Merry Widow (A Lorne Simpkins short story)

It's A Dog's Life (A Lorne Simpkins short story)

A Time To Heal (A Sweet Romance)

A Time For Change (A Sweet Romance)

High Spirits

The Temptation series (Romantic Suspense/New Adult Novellas)

Past Temptation

Lost Temptation

Clever Deception (co-written by Linda S Prather)

Tragic Deception (co-written by Linda S Prather)

Sinful Deception (co-written by Linda S Prather)

# PROLOGUE

The group of boys, up to mischief as usual, were playing down by what used to be the lake, until the drought had struck. Now it resembled a small patch of water, barely bigger than a large puddle.

"Will you look at that? I've never seen it so low," Danny Murphy said.

"Get on with it, Danny. Who cares? It doesn't concern us," Titch replied. He kicked out at a nearby stone. Normally it would have made a loud splash as it dropped into the water, but not today.

Danny shook his head. His parents had sat him down the evening before and given him a lengthy lecture about him not wasting water during the drought, otherwise they could be the ones facing a fine. Titch's parents hadn't bothered going down the same route with him. "It should do. You know what's expected of us during the drought, don't ya?"

Titch shrugged and pulled a face. "My ma did warn me, but I couldn't give a sodding rat's arse. Get the damn ball, will ya? It's over there."

"Jesus, why me? You go. I hate the thought of treading

across this cracked earth, you never know what is lying in there. It's caked around the edges, but where the ball is, you can tell it's all muddy. It's your ball, you get it."

"Hopeless, that's what you are." Titch wrenched on Danny's arm to get past him and proceeded to tiptoe across the hard surface.

Danny and the other two boys, Zig and Zag as they were nicknamed, watched on as he picked his way out to the middle of what used to be the deep lake to retrieve the ball.

"Scaredy cats. It's fine, you're worried about nothing." Titch inched closer to the ball. His foot sank in a clump of mud close to the ball. It was within reach now, but then, so was something else. Titch called out to the others, "Hey, over 'ere. What do you reckon this is? Come on, it's safe, I've proved that."

The three other boys crossed the craggy surface towards Titch. He waited for them to arrive, unsure what he had stumbled across.

"What's that?" Zig asked.

"Is it a sack?" Zag asked.

The sack was stuck in the mud, most of it still embedded in the sludge. "Why don't we leave it?" Danny muttered. "It's not doing any harm, is it?"

"Don't you want to know what's inside, mate?"

"Not really. All I want to do is get the fuck out of here. My folks have warned me about playing down here, by the lake and along the riverbanks. The same as your folks have. There's no point in any of you denying it, you all told me so last year."

Titch roared. "Lake? This can't be classed as one of them, not now. Look around ya."

"I am, and it's scaring the shit out of me."

"You act all macho when you're at school but you're nothing but a bloody coward when you're with us."

"Get stuffed. This place is freaking me out, what about you boys?" Danny asked Zig and Zag.

They shrugged in response.

Titch mumbled something indecipherable and ventured across the mud, not worried if his feet sank deeper or what his mum would say when she saw the state his trainers were in when he returned home. "Nearly there. It would be great if I got some help."

Zig stepped forward to join him.

"Cheers, mate. Why don't we both grab the bag and pull it out together?"

"I've got a better idea. Why don't we just leave it where it is and open it? Otherwise, we're going to get in a right mess."

"Yeah, that's a good shout. Okay, stay there. I'm mucky anyhow, I might as well be the one who opens the bag." Titch took another few tentative steps towards the mud-encrusted hessian sack and tugged on the tie at the top. It was one of those plastic zip ties, but it refused to budge. "No good. I'm going to have to tear the sack open."

"Be careful, Titch," Zig shouted.

"Don't say it like that, it's only a sack, for fuck's sake."

"I know, it's what's on the inside that I'm worried about."

Titch took a penknife from his pocket, the one his grandfather had given him for Christmas, without his mother knowing, and slit a four-inch hole in the side of the bag and stepped back. He wasn't sure what he'd been expecting to break free. The anticipation had his heart pounding against his ribs.

"Go on, what's inside?" Zig asked, his neck strained, but he was still a fair way back compared to Titch.

"I can't make it out. I'm going to have to get closer. Come with me, Zig, don't hold back."

"I... I shouldn't, not really. These trainers were only

bought last week, and Mum threatened she'd do all sorts to me if I mess them up today."

"Yeah, right. Spouting the same old crap you usually come out with."

"I ain't. It's the truth. Ask Zag if you don't believe me."

"It's true, Titch, I was there all right," Zag called from behind Titch.

"Fuck! If you want anything doing…" Titch took another hesitant step towards the sack and crouched beside it. The cut wasn't long enough, so he ripped the bag open until the tear was over ten inches. Something slipped through the gap. After the initial shock, Titch shuffled closer to have a better look and caught a glimpse of what appeared to be a skull. He scampered backwards at speed. Getting to his feet, he left Zig standing there.

"Hey, what the shit, man? What's going on?" Zig stared at the bag, hoping to get a better look. It was impossible to see from where he was standing. He shuffled forward, caught a glimpse of the skull and the rest of the bones inside the sack, then bolted after Titch.

They caught up with the other boys, all four of them by now petrified and flummoxed about what to do next.

"What the hell was in there?" Danny asked.

Titch swallowed down the acid burning his throat. "A dead body."

"Shit!" Danny ran, and the others followed him.

They hadn't got far when they literally bumped into a man in his fifties, walking his Labrador along the parched path.

"Oi, what are you four up to?"

Titch glanced over his shoulder and pointed, his finger visibly shaking. "It's back there."

"What is?" The man's gaze tried to follow Titch's finger.

"A dead… body… We've gotta get out of here, mister, don't make us stay around," Titch pleaded.

"Tell me where it is exactly and then you can go."

"Just on the edge of the water in a hessian sack. We're outta here."

The four of them took off, leaving the man gaping.

# CHAPTER 1

"We've just received a call from the desk sergeant, boss," Joanna Tryst said.

Sally immediately walked across the room and stood beside her colleague. "I'm all ears. What's going on?"

"A member of the public has contacted the station to report the sighting of human remains down by Cavendish Lake."

"Okay, do we have any further details on the victim, Joanna?"

She shrugged. "That's as much as I've been given. Sorry."

"Hang on a minute," Jack said. "Why are we getting involved in this? We're a cold case team."

Sally raised an eyebrow at her partner. "I should imagine because the remains aren't in good shape. We won't know until we get there, will we, Jack?"

He held his hands up. "I was just checking. Wouldn't want us going out there on a wasted trip now, would I?"

"We'll head over there now, Joanna. Lorne, you're in charge while we're out. Let's see if we can't tie up all these ongoing cases this week. I've had it up to here with trawling through the same crap DI Falkirk wrote up as notes for all these deplorable crimes."

"I think we're well on the way to achieving that goal, boss," Lorne replied.

Sally's smile reflected her relief. "Good to hear. It's been a hell of a job, but to stumble across that little ray of light at the end of the tunnel is music to my ears. Right, come on, Jack, let's get our skates on. We'll be in touch with an update soon, guys. In the meantime, heads down and crack on."

She collected her keys from her office, and Jack followed her down the stairs and through the reception area.

"We're on the case, Pat," Sally said to the desk sergeant. "Have your guys secured the crime scene, and has the pathologist been informed?"

"All in hand, DI Parker."

"Excellent news."

THE DRIVE OUT to the scene was filled with tension. Jack knew when to remain quiet, to leave Sally to her thoughts. She drew up alongside the patrol car and took the decision to get suited up right away.

"Why? What's the point if it's a cold case?" Jack asked.

"I can't believe you said that. Every case needs to be treated the same. Just do it, Bullet."

He huffed and puffed and hitched the suit over his bulky frame. Jack was ex-military, who carried several scars to prove he'd had a rough deal in the army. The scars had also given him the nickname Bullet, which Sally tended to only use when she was narked with him.

Once they were togged up, they dipped under the cordon and signed the Crime Scene Log. They found a young male officer standing around ten feet away from the remains.

He smiled and gave a brief nod. "Morning, ma'am, sir. Another gruesome discovery for you to investigate."

"Apparently so. Any news on the pathologist yet?"

"On the way, ma'am. Should be here soon. She asked me to make sure no one approached the remains until she got here."

Sally nodded. "Fair enough. I wouldn't want to step on the new girl's toes."

"How's Simon enjoying his freedom nowadays?" Jack asked.

Simon, the former pathologist, and Sally's husband, had taken early retirement, bored with cutting up bodies and dealing with bureaucratic paperwork. Now, he was a full-time property developer, something he'd dabbled in for the last few years, in partnership with Sally's father. Sadly, her father had suffered a run of bad health, forcing him to retire. Rather than give up their lucrative business, Simon had decided to throw in the towel on his old career and thrust himself headlong into being a property developer alongside Lorne's husband, Tony. Although, Tony's position was part-time at present, because he and Lorne had the kennels to run as well. Altogether, they were very busy bees, both on and off the force, as well as good friends and neighbours.

"He's enjoying it so far. Still keeps an eye on what's going on through the medical journals et cetera. Who knows if he'll miss the smell of dead bodies in the future, or not? I suppose it depends on how successful he is as a developer."

"Yuck... Tough call these days, the price of materials increasing rapidly and property prices going through the roof."

"Yep, plus we have no idea if we're heading into a recession or not. It's on the cards."

"Yeah, so they say. That's going to ultimately affect the property values. I'm old enough to remember the last time we dipped into a recession. The number of people who ended up in negative equity, and were forced to sell because they could no longer afford to pay the bills on their homes was appalling. This government needs shooting if they allow that kind of thing to happen again. A vast contrast to keeping the housing market going during the lockdown when they adjusted the stamp duty, knocking it on the head for the lower end of the market. House prices rose at a phenomenal rate, and now look where we are."

Sally stared at him. "I didn't realise you were such an expert, Jack."

"I'm not. I'm a homeowner whose mortgage rates have ebbed and flowed over the last few years, that's all. If that makes me an expert, then so be it."

"I can see troubled times ahead for a lot of people, and it's not only the government that needs a rocket up their backsides, it's the energy companies as well."

"You should be all right on that front. Haven't you just had solar panels fitted?"

"Yep, it was Simon's idea. I was dead set against it to begin with but even I have to admit it has been a godsend. I think they're going to make a huge difference to our energy bills in the winter. I hope we have a mild one ahead of us. I fear for the pensioners and people on limited incomes and how they're going to cope otherwise."

"All doom and gloom, one way or another this year, now we're in the middle of this damn drought. It's as though someone up there is throwing all this shit at us, testing us."

"Possibly." Sally cast an eye over her right shoulder. "I remember coming here as a kid. Never seen it this dry before, have you?"

"Never. I'm horrified to see it in such a state. Breaks my heart to think what lies ahead of us. Too many governments have ignored the issue of climate change over the years, and now this is the result. In a few weeks, I bet we'll be suffering from floods, you mark my words."

"We're a miserable pair of fuckers, aren't we?"

Their attention was drawn back to the car park where a van pulled up.

"Is this her?" Jack asked out of the corner of his mouth.

"I think so. I can't make out what she's like yet, can you? Is she young or old?"

"It depends on what you class as 'young'. She'd have eight years of training behind her, minimum." He peered closer and confirmed, "She looks old to me, well, about your age anyway."

The unkind and uncalled for jibe earnt him a dig in the ribs. "You've got a bloody nerve. Hey, you, you're forgetting something, you're eleven years older than me."

He cringed. "All right, there's no need for you to take pleasure in telling me what I already know."

"So, what you're effectively saying is, that I'm old but you're *ancient*. Ah, right, I've got you."

He chuntered and turned his head away.

Sally stroked her finger in the air. "Strike one for the week, bring on the rest of them."

The pathologist took her time, methodically getting her bag of equipment out of the back of the van before she crossed the arid soil to join them.

"Are you the officer in charge?" she asked, her question aimed at Jack.

He jerked a thumb in Sally's direction. "DI Parker is."

Sally smiled at the woman whose cheeks had coloured up under her gaze.

"Ouch! Not a good start on my part. Sorry for the misguided presumption. I just thought as the gent was older... it had nothing to do with you being a woman... Shall I stop digging now?"

Sally laughed. "Don't worry about it, it was an easy mistake to make. I'm Sally Parker. This is my partner, DS Jack Blackman. And you are?"

"The person who has taken over your husband's role, if I'm not mistaken?"

"You're not. Welcome, how's the job going so far?"

"Ah, you're not going to catch me out there."

Sally frowned and inclined her head. "Sorry?"

"Don't tell me you're not the type to go back to your husband and tell him tittle-tattle about his successor."

"I'm not. I promise. It was a genuine question. We seem to have got off on the wrong foot."

"Do we? We're both entitled to our opinion. You'll learn that about me in the months ahead. I don't hold back, speak my mind, but never take offence if someone counters with a different point of view."

"I'm pretty much the same."

"Bullshit," Jack said as he coughed, earning himself a stamp on the foot.

"Ignore my partner, he can be a first-rate goon at times."

"I will. Right, do you two want to lead the way? You didn't mind me giving instructions for you not to approach the crime scene, did you?"

"No. If that's the way you want to play it, it's fine by me. I'd rather take a look at the findings as and when you're on the scene," Sally added.

"Onwards then."

"Are you from around this area?" Sally asked. "Sorry, I didn't catch your name?"

"I didn't give it. Very remiss of me, eager to get on with the job in hand. I'm Pauline Quick, you can call me Paul, if you want, I don't mind. No, I've never worked in the Norfolk area before, although I've visited here on a few occasions. I grew up just over the border in Suffolk, so not too far for me to relocate here."

"Ah, I see. So you've set up home here now, I take it?"

"Yes. In Thetford. I'm renting at present, until I can find somewhere closer to the mortuary. Always difficult at this time of the year, what with it being in the middle of the holiday season."

"Yes, we're inundated at the moment, that's true. I hope you find somewhere more permanent soon."

"No doubt I will. Is this common, to have the lakes around here dry up like this in the summer?"

"No, this is exceptional, quite the opposite normally. Drought conditions, the type that hasn't been seen for donkey's years. Even the rivers are really low at present. Lots of pleasure boats going to ground in the narrower stretches of the Broads."

"That's a shame for the holidaymakers but also for the businesses running the boats. Unprecedented times we're living in. Not sure where it's going to end, are you?"

"My partner and I were just having the same conversation whilst waiting for you to arrive."

"Who made the discovery, any idea?"

Sally mentally kicked herself for not asking the constable they'd first spoken to at the scene. "I'll ask the PC in a second. There was no one else around when we got here."

"Do you take bets?" Pauline asked.

"Not really. Why?"

"I'm thinking it was probably a dog walker. It always is, isn't it?"

Sally laughed. "More often than I care to mention."

"Let's proceed, nonetheless. Maybe we should count ourselves lucky the drought has struck," Pauline suggested as they inched ever closer to the sack.

"I wonder how long it has been in the lake. Will you be able to give us that information?"

"Not for a while. A handful of tests will need to be carried out before I can divulge anything as accurate as that. I will also need to reach out to some other experienced professionals in the field. Laying my cards on the table, not wishing to put you off me at this early stage, but just giving you fair warning that I've never had to deal with a body being dumped in a lake before. There are various contributing factors that will need to be considered before I'll be able to present you with any definitive answers."

"I get that." Sally smiled and nodded. "But if you can push things along for us, you and I will soon become the best of friends."

Pauline laughed. "Is that how you ended up marrying my predecessor, laying that kind of deal on the table?"

Jack sniggered and turned his back on them.

For a moment, Sally struggled to answer the direct question. "I… umm… I suppose… Umm…"

Pauline patted Sally on the shoulder and winked at her. "Never mind, I was only winding you up. Sorry if you felt it was in poor taste and made you feel uncomfortable."

"It didn't, although I sense my partner is thinking differently."

Pauline knelt in the muddy patch next to the sack, not batting an eye about what state her protective suit would be in when she stood again.

*That's what it's there for, I suppose.*

"Hmm… I'm going to need to wait until the team arrive before I shift the sack."

"This might sound a silly question," Sally began, "but can you give us a clue about this person's gender?" She immediately chewed on her lip after Pauline glanced up and raised a surprised eyebrow. Sally wagged her finger. "Yeah, dumb question, I know. Ignore me. I have a tendency to speak before I've engaged my brain, now and again. This was one such occasion." She caught Jack's shoulders doing a jig beside her and wished she was three steps closer so she could wipe the smug grin off his face.

"Let's call it an obvious question but one I don't have an answer to just now, how's that?"

"Thank you for being so tactful and for not embarrassing me further, Pauline."

"You're welcome. DS Blackman, would you mind fetching the piece of tarpaulin I have rolled up in the back of the van? It's on the left."

"Sure, I'll be right back." Jack set off, picking a route through the craggy earth.

"I felt you needed the time to recover without your partner hanging around, relishing your embarrassment," Pauline said.

"Don't worry about me, Jack's one of the good ones. I'm just as comfortable about him winding me up as I am at pulling his leg. It doesn't take much to amuse him when I make a blunder either. It's all good, I promise you."

"Glad to hear it. I see so many women treated appallingly by their male counterparts in the force these days, I like to do my bit by checking the female officer is okay before I let rip at someone. I, too, have a problem with engaging my brain before my mouth at times."

Sally smiled. "I think we're going to get on just great and I hear you on the misogyny, too. I thought we'd seen the last of it a few years ago but from what I can tell there has been a resurgence of it lately that needs to be stamped out. Thankfully, I haven't seen any of it around our station."

"It's worth keeping an eye open for. If it creeps back in then we have a duty to blow the whistle on the culprit right away."

"Don't worry, I work with a group of very strong women. None of us would put up with such crap."

"What crap?" Jack asked.

Sally had been so caught up in the topic she and Pauline had been discussing, she had failed to hear her partner return. "Nothing, just general women's chitchat."

Jack placed the tarp on the ground next to the sack and stood back. "Ah, you mean gossiping, don't you?"

Sally gave him 'the look', and he grinned broadly.

He thumbed behind him. "In case you hadn't noticed, SOCO have arrived."

"Thanks, I had," Pauline replied. She glanced beyond him at the cars and beckoned the technicians, urging them to get a move on.

Sally was impressed by the team's rapid movements as they collected their gear and their willingness to join them quickly. "By the look of things, you've got them wrapped around your finger already."

"I believe in having an open relationship with my work colleagues. We had a meeting on my first day in which I laid down my rules. It sounds bad, but it wasn't really. I've experienced a great deal of backlash in my previous roles. This way, everyone knows the standard of work I expect from the outset. Some might call me a hard bitch. I'd prefer to call it getting the job done in the swiftest way possible, without the need for stepping on anyone's toes."

"I'm with you there. It's best to be forthright about your expectations from the get-go. They appear to be adhering to your wishes well."

Pauline winked. "So far so good. Here they come now. If you and Jack wouldn't mind stepping back for a few moments while I give the team their instructions, we should have this place cleared within a few hours."

"Sounds good to me. The sooner we get to ID the victim

the better. I'll have another chat with the PC about the witness and come back to you in five."

Sally and Jack passed the SOCO team on the way.

"All right, chaps?" Sally asked.

"Nice to see you again, Inspector, shame about the circumstances. I see you've met Simon's replacement," Barry said.

"We have. We won't hold you up, she's eager to get on with it, which is fine by me."

The team continued on their journey with an odd smile here and there amongst them.

"They seem happy enough. What do you make of her?" Jack asked. "A sharp contrast to dealing with Simon on the job, eh?"

"Each to their own," Sally said. "Everyone has a different way of getting the job done. I'm happy with the way she appears to be handling it. Only time will tell if I'll live to regret those words or not."

"Yeah, okay. I hope we don't."

"What's your impression of her?" Sally asked just before they reached the PC.

"I'm on the fence, shall we say. At the moment she seems fine. My doubts will probably come when we start badgering her for answers."

"Maybe we won't have to, have you thought about that?"

"We'll see."

The PC turned to face them as they arrived.

"Hi again. I forgot to ask who found the remains," Sally said, her eye drawn back to the parked vehicles, in case she had missed anyone lingering there.

The officer removed his notebook from his pocket and flipped it open. Jack did the same in readiness to jot down the details.

"He couldn't hang around, had an appointment at the

dentist he needed to attend, ma'am. I said that was fine and I'd pass on his details to the officer in charge once you arrived. His name is Bert Mead. His address is forty Lockyer Close, Kimberley. Just up the road there."

"How long will he be held up at the dentist's, any idea?"

"He said it was a general checkup and hygienist appointment and that he should be back home within the hour. That was around fifty minutes ago."

"We'll do the necessary here and then drop by and see him. How did he seem to you?"

"A bit shaken up. I've seen people in a worse state, however, in the circumstances."

"Good to know, thanks. Did you see anyone else hanging around when you got here?"

"No, only Mr Mead. Always better not to have a crowd to deal with, eh, Inspector?"

"A bonus right enough. Thanks again."

Once more, Sally and Jack made their way across the arid, often crater-like terrain, to rejoin Pauline and her team. Sally decided to watch the proceedings from a few feet back, giving the team room to remove the bones from the sack. Sally cringed. There was something about seeing the skeletal remains of a human being that sent shivers down her spine at a crime scene. And yet, she had never had a problem when she had viewed a skeleton at school in the biology lab.

Jack's impatience grew, and he kicked out at the earth, sending small stones spiralling into the deep cracks. Sally's interest remained focused on how Pauline and her team were performing.

"What's that?" she asked.

"There are a few items of clothing, or remnants of such, and this." Pauline held up a piece of rusted metal.

"A badge of sorts?" Sally asked, straining to get a closer view of the item.

"Isn't it a belt buckle?" Jack suggested.

Pauline nodded. "I'm inclined to agree with Jack. It's pretty distinctive. As soon as we get back to the lab, I'll put a member of the team on it, see if we can get it cleaned up. You never know, it might help us identify the victim."

"Good call. Is it too soon to ask if the victim is male or female?" Sally asked.

Pauline paused and scanned the area surrounding them as she thought. "I'm going out on a limb here, I won't be able to give you a definitive answer until we have all the bones assembled and carry out the measurements, but a rough guess would be that we're looking at a female."

Sally's heart lurched. "Bummer. Not that it matters either way. Do women tend to wear belt buckles, though?"

"Donna does," Jack butted in, referring to his wife. "Occasionally, when she wears a certain pair of jeans that she loves to wear but are a size too big now she's lost some weight."

"I've been known to as well," Pauline admitted.

Sally shrugged. "I've never felt the need to. Each to their own, I guess. Is there anything else in the sack?"

Pauline searched with gloved hands and pulled out several pieces of cloth. "Only these and a few heavy stones. I'm presuming they were to weigh the sack down."

"Sounds about right. I hate to pressure you, Pauline, I'm not the type, but how long do you think it's going to be before you can give us any information about the deceased?"

Pauline glanced up and smiled. "Shame I haven't got a crystal ball handy."

"Oh well. It was worth a punt. A few days? Weeks?"

"If you're going to push me, I'd be more inclined to say weeks. Of course, it depends on what other cases arise in between, which might take priority."

Sally nodded, her mood dipping considerably at the news,

even though she'd been half expecting the pathologist to say as much. "Do you have my number?"

"I think I saw one of your cards on my desk, obviously left there by your husband. I'll be in touch as soon as I can. In the meantime, if anything substantial comes to light, I'll let you know right away. Until then, I'm going to have to ask you to have the patience of a saint."

"I hear you. I'll give you one of my cards just in case you've ditched the other one. I can't wait to hear what you can tell me about the victim, in your own time, of course. No pressure from me. We'll shoot off and see what the witness has to say."

"Fine by me. We could be here a while yet. Good luck."

"You, too. Take care of her or him."

Pauline nodded. "They're in good hands with us, I assure you."

Sally and Jack left the area and removed their paper suits, which they deposited in the awaiting black bag at the edge of the cordon, then they walked back to the car.

"Over to see the witness now, I take it?" Jack asked.

"Correct. Odds are that he won't be able to tell us much, but it's a necessity."


THEY PULLED up outside a small terraced house on the outskirts of the village. It had a pretty cottage garden at the front, as did all the other houses in the row.

"Looks like they're in competition with each other," Jack noted.

"Perhaps they've entered Britain in Bloom. Is that still going?"

Jack stared at her over the roof of the car. "What are you asking me for? I'm no gardener."

"Simple question, partner, no need to snap my head off."

"Don't pull that one, I didn't."

"Let's agree to disagree on that point, shall we?"

"Okay."

Sally locked the car and walked up the winding, block-paved path to the front door and rang the bell. She fed a hand into her pocket and removed her warrant card.

A man in his mid-to-late fifties opened the door a few seconds later. A dog barked in the hallway behind him. "Hush now. Go inside. Sorry about that, overprotective at the best of times, that one."

Sally held up her ID and smiled. "Not a problem. Are you Mr Mead? I'm DI Sally Parker, and this is my partner, DS Jack Blackman."

"I am. Ah, the police, I've been expecting someone to stop by and see me. Let me put the dog in the kitchen. Come in."

Sally entered the house as he tussled with the golden Labrador to get him into the kitchen. The dog reminded her of her own dog, Dex. He was now living with her and Simon permanently, instead of with Sally's parents, thanks to Simon's new work regime. Dex spent most of the time in the car, travelling around the building sites Simon had on the go at present.

Mr Mead returned and opened the door to the lounge. "Come through."

"I have a Lab, too. Isn't yours good with strangers?"

"He has his moments. Most of the time he's fine. I had to take him to the vet's last week, and they've found a lump that needs further investigation. I'm putting his slight aggression down to the change in his health, although who knows when they get to his age? He's nearly twelve now."

"Ah, it's always tough as they get older. Mine is nearly nine, still a puppy at times, but I can see the grey appearing on his muzzle and catch him walking slowly around the garden now and again. Fortunately, his appetite is good most days, which is usually a telling sign if there's anything medically wrong with them."

"Hang on to the good times. I'm not sure what I'm going to do if I lose Bruno, he's all I've got. I had to take early retirement from the army because of PTSD. It's quite mild, but still there, nevertheless. Please take a seat. Sorry, where are my manners? Can I get you a tea or coffee?"

Sally raised a finger. "It's okay. We shouldn't keep you too long."

She sat on the worn brown sofa next to Jack, and Mr Mead sat opposite them in a reclining leather armchair.

"If you can tell us what happened when you discovered… the body today," she said.

"Ah, yes, of course. Well, I was down at what used to be the lake. Never seen it so low in all my years of living around here. Of course, I used to be away a lot of the time with the army. Anyway, you don't want to hear about all of that. I was walking Bruno around the lake as usual when four young boys came hurtling my way. They seemed terrified, and I held out a hand to stop them to ask what was going on. One of them managed to get out that they had found a body in the lake."

"Ah, I see. So it wasn't really you who discovered the remains, as such, then?"

"No. Honestly, the boys were so petrified, I told them to skedaddle and get themselves home and that I would deal with the police. Sorry if I've done the wrong thing."

"You haven't. Had the discovery been that of someone who had passed away recently then I might have been a tad upset. I'm sure given the length of time the body was in the water, no harm has been done. I'm not surprised the boys were petrified and running away from the scene when you came across them."

"I took a closer look before ringing nine-nine-nine just to

make sure what it was. It would have been embarrassing to have rung you if there hadn't been anything down there. You know what furtive imaginations children have. Imagine my surprise when I discovered they were telling the truth." He shook his head and ran a hand over his face. "I saw a lot of dead bodies during my army days but I've never stumbled across a skeleton before."

"It's a chilling experience, isn't it?"

"And some. Made the hairs on the back of my neck stand on end, I can tell you. Any idea who the victim is? Will you even be able to tell who it is?"

"It's going to take time. The pathologist and her team are at the scene now. I can't see us getting anywhere anytime soon. I have to ask if there was anyone else hanging around down at the lake when you got there."

"The odd walker on the other side, no one close to where the sack was discovered. You think the killer might be hanging around? Sounds inconceivable to me."

"It's something I need to ask. We have no idea how long the sack has been there. For all we know, someone might have dumped it down there within the last few days."

"Ah, I never thought about that aspect. I suppose it's a possibility. No, there was no one near there, from what I could see, apart from the boys, me and Bruno."

"It's a mysterious one for sure. Oh well, we're going to need to get a statement from you in the next day or two. Would it be okay if I passed on your details to the desk sergeant? He'll arrange for a constable to come out and see you at a time convenient to you."

"That's fine. Any time suits me. I'll give you my mobile number, just in case I'm out walking Bruno."

Jack wrote down the number he gave them in his notebook, then Sally and Jack got to their feet, ready to leave.

"Thanks for your help," Sally said. "We'll be in touch soon."

He showed them out into the hallway. "I hope you find justice for the person in the sack. What a despicable way to go, eh?"

"It is. Fingers crossed. I see a lot of work ahead of us during this investigation. Nice meeting you. Take care."

"You, too."

He closed the door gently behind them.

"I sense this case is going to have us pulling our hair out soon enough," Jack mumbled on the way back to the car.

"We're going to need to dig deep and think positive at all times."

They settled in the car and began the journey back to the station. Halfway through the trip, Jack received a call on his mobile. Sally did her best to switch off from his personal conversation, however, his sudden silence caused her concern. She pulled over and turned his way. All traces of colour had drained from his face.

"Jack? Are you all right?"

He stared at her, his eyes bulging with tears, and shook his head.

Sally took the phone from his hand. "Hello, this is DI Sally Parker. To whom am I speaking?"

"Sally, it's me, Donna. Is Jack all right?"

"No. What's going on, Donna? He looks like he's in shock."

Jack's wife broke down in tears. "It's his dad. He's been killed in a car crash down south."

"Oh my God, I'm so sorry to hear that." Sally squeezed Jack's hand; he just stared at her in deep shock. "What do you need me to do, Donna? Are you okay?"

"I'm worried about Jack, they were really close. We were

due to visit him in a couple of weeks. I don't know what to do for the best. Did I do the right thing telling him?"

"Yes, of course. Leave it with me. We're on our way back to the station now. I'll sort things there. You take care of yourself. Jack's in safe hands with me."

"Thanks, Sally. Should I tell the girls or leave it until Jack comes home?"

"I would leave it for now. Sending hugs."

Donna ended the call, and Sally reached over to give her partner a hug.

He remained rigid in her arms and whispered, "I can't believe it. We were going down to see him… in a few weeks, and now… he's… gone."

"I have no words to offer you, Jack. I'm as shocked as you are about this. We should get back to the station, unless you want to stop off somewhere and have a quick shot to soften the blow?"

He considered the options for a second or two then shook his head. "Preferably the last one, but I value my career, and it would just be my luck if we got caught. Bloody hell… I know Dad was getting on a bit, but I thought he'd be around for a few more years yet."

"How old was he?"

"Sixty-eight. That's not old these days, is it?"

"I wonder what happened. Donna didn't really fill me in. Not that it matters. Jesus, let's get you back to the station." Sally started the engine again and indicated into the flow of traffic.

Jack continued to stare straight ahead of him, intermittently either sighing or shaking his head in disbelief. Sally was struck dumb. What did one say in such circumstances? Jack knew her sympathies lay with him, but it didn't stop her feeling numb and totally inadequate.

After Sally parked the car in her allotted space, they entered the station. Pat was desperate to get Sally's attention. She stopped in reception long enough to tell Jack to go on ahead and then made her way over to the counter to speak with Pat.

"Is something wrong, ma'am?"

Sally shrugged. "The worst news possible. Jack has just been told his father has died in a car accident. Don't ask... that's all we know."

"Shit! That's terrible. Poor Jack."

"I can't hang around for long, for obvious reasons. What do you need, Pat?"

"I wanted to tell you that I've arranged for a female officer to go round and take a statement from the witness, Mr Mead."

"Wonderful. I was going to request that when we got back. Not that he managed to tell us much. In truth, he wasn't the one who discovered the remains, four young boys did. He told them to get home because they were shaken up pretty badly and he hung around until the patrol car got to the scene."

"Sounds a decent enough chap. I'm not surprised the kids were distraught. Want me to see if I can try and trace them for you?"

Sally shook her head and wrinkled her nose. "I can't see much point in speaking with them, they found the remains and legged it. What else is there to tell? It'll only be a waste of resources and also put the fear of God into the kids if the coppers show up at their front doors. Not worth the hassle with the parents, is it? Anyway, I'd better get on and see how Jack is. I'll leave the statement in your capable hands."

"You do that. Give Jack my condolences. Should he be here?"

"I'm going to send him on his way but need him to get his

head straight first. I can do without him being in an accident of his own."

"I'm with you. It's one of those issues where you don't know what to do for the best, isn't it?"

"Too right." Sally entered her security number into the keypad, and the door opened. She trudged her way up the stairs, distracted, her mind racing with dozens of questions about how she was supposed to handle her partner's issue without putting her foot in it.

At the top of the stairs, she bumped into DCI Mick Green.

"Hey, what's going on, Sally?"

She took a step back on the landing and shook her head. "I wish I knew."

His eyebrow cocked, he said, "You're going to have to give me more than that. What's happened?"

She sighed and revealed the truth. He guided her to the side of the landing, out of the way of other detectives milling around, and flopped against the wall. "Jesus! Is he all right? Has he gone home?"

"No. He's still here. I thought it best rather than allowing him to drive. As you can imagine, the news has floored him."

"Well, of course it has. Do you want me to have a word with him? There are procedures in place for compassionate leave."

"I wondered if that might be the case. He's going to need time off as his father lived further down south, although I'm not completely sure where."

"You didn't answer me, do you want me to have a word with him?"

Sally nodded. "Yes, if you don't mind. I suddenly feel out of my depth, maybe because I'm too close to him."

"It's fine. I'll speak to him in your office. It'll come across as less formal as opposed to me summoning him to mine, if that's agreeable with you?"

"Go for it. I'm still in a state of shock myself, can't imagine what's going through his mind right now."

"Leave it with me. I had to deal with something along these lines a few years ago when I was a DI. Unfortunately, I had to tell a member of my team his mother had been knifed by an armed burglar who had got into her home."

"How terrible. How did you cope with the undertaking?"

He shrugged. "You just do. You have to switch off your own feelings and put the person you're dealing with first. Leave it with me. I wouldn't exactly call myself a dab hand at this sort of thing, but I think I have more experience than you, by the look of things."

"Then I'm happy for you to take over. Be gentle with him."

He tutted and walked ahead of her into the main office. Jack was at his desk, staring at the wall ahead of him. The rest of the team all seemed confused and unsure what to say or do.

Mick Green crossed the room and placed a hand on Jack's shoulder. He glanced up and fidgeted in his chair.

"Come with me, Jack."

Her partner shot out of his chair and followed the DCI into Sally's office. Once the door was closed, she perched on the desk behind her and exhaled a large breath.

Lorne approached her. "You look like you're in need of a coffee."

Sally smiled. "Thanks."

Lorne returned from the drinks station with a cup in each hand. "Dare I ask what's going on?"

"Thanks. Hasn't Jack said anything?"

"No. He came in, a few of us called out hello, he ignored us and plonked down at the desk with his head in his hands. I was concerned something had happened to you but I'm relieved to see you're okay. What's going on?"

"It's his dad, he's been killed in an accident. Don't ask me any more than that, we don't have any further details. I think I'm as shocked as he is. I thought it best if he came back here rather than get in the car and drive straight home. Not sure if that was the right call or not. I literally bumped into DCI Green outside, he said he'd have a word with Jack."

"He'll be in there now, ensuring Jack is okay to drive before letting him go. He's going to need to take compassionate leave, too. Not ideal with a new case landing on the table."

Sally nodded. "I know. However, that's the least of our worries. You're going to have to step in and fill his shoes for a while."

Lorne's hand covered her chest. "Me? What about the others? Won't me jumping in to become your partner put their backs up?"

"Not at all. They're a good team, they'll understand the reasons behind my decision. You have a vast amount of experience compared to the rest of them. That's not putting the others down, it just makes sense to me."

Lorne's expression turned thoughtful. After a while, she whispered, "I just wouldn't feel right, Sally. You know me, I try to avoid any kind of conflict."

As well as being her colleague, Lorne was one of her best friends. They even lived close to each other and had a gate at the bottom of their gardens, connecting their homes. "If it comes to it, I would much prefer you to be my wingman, Lorne. Don't let me down."

A glimmer of a smile lit up Lorne's face, and she sipped at her coffee. Before she had a chance to respond, the door to Sally's office opened, and DCI Green came out, without Jack.

Sally left Lorne and crossed the room to join him. "Is he all right?"

"Yes, I've left him gathering his thoughts for a moment. He's going home. I've told him one of the guys will give him a lift, but he insisted he can manage. He just needs a few more minutes for the truth to sink in properly. I'm sure he's going to be okay. He's officially entitled to three to five days bereavement leave. I've told him to take as long as he needs and we'll work around it. I'm aware he's not the type to take the piss. Meanwhile, that leaves you a man down with an important case on your hands." His gaze immediately shifted in Lorne's direction.

"I've just asked, and she's reluctant to take on the role in case it upsets the others, what with her being the newcomer to the team."

"Bollocks," he muttered and walked across the room to speak with Lorne. "How are you getting on, DS Warner?"

Lorne's gaze flicked between Sally and DCI Green. "I think I've fitted in well, thanks for asking, sir."

"Good. You're aware of what's come up. DI Parker and I have discussed what needs to happen. We've agreed you should become her partner for the next week or so, until Jack returns to work."

"But… I…"

"Good, that's settled. As you were, team, I have to fly. I have a Zoom meeting taking place within the next five minutes. Good luck with the new investigation. I'll expect regular updates as per usual, DI Parker."

"Yes, sir." Sally moved to stand alongside Lorne and nudged her. "It'll be like the old days."

"I can't help but feel I've been hoodwinked into accepting my new role, *partner*. What will Jack think when he hears?"

"He'll be thrilled." Sally chewed her lower lip. "Maybe the

wrong term to use in the circumstances. I'm sure he'll be fine, just like the rest of the team. You worry too much."

"My only hesitation is that he'll think I'm taking over. Anyway, what about the case I'm working on with Jordan? Or had you forgotten that?"

"I hadn't. You won't be exclusively working with me, possibly ninety percent of the time, hence you'll still be able to give Jordan a hand, how's that?"

Lorne groaned. "Sounds like a lot of hard work landing on my shoulders if you ask me."

"You can cope. We're all going to have to play our part, what with us being a man down."

Just then, the door to the office opened, and a tearful-looking Jack came into the room.

"We'll discuss this more later. I need to check on him." Sally raced over to speak with Jack. "How are you?"

"I'm okay. Getting used to the idea now. DCI Green said I could take time off, if that's okay with you? I feel bad, letting you down, what with the new case landing on us."

"Don't feel bad, Jack. Family comes first, always. Do you need a lift?"

"I thought about it; I don't think so. All right if I get off now? Donna will be narked with me if I hang around here much longer, ignoring her needs. She was really close to my dad, and we're going to have to sit down and tell the girls today, as well. No idea how they're going to take it. I mean, Teresa will be okay, what with her being twenty-two now, Diane will be a different story, and then there's Teresa's little one, Mary Rose, to consider. This will be the first death in the family she's had to deal with…"

"The right words will come to you when you're ready to share with them, Jack. Don't put too much pressure on yourself. Hey, I'm always at the end of the phone, too. Don't ever forget it."

"I won't. Thanks, boss."

Sally patted his arm. "You go, with the team's best wishes. Again, sorry for your loss. Will you keep in touch? Let me know how it happened… no, on second thoughts, ignore that, you're going to have enough on your plate to deal with as it is."

"So are you. I suppose Lorne will become your partner, temporarily, won't she?"

Sally didn't pick up on any malice in his words. "DCI Green asked her to do just that before he left. I think Lorne feels a tad uncomfortable and is going to need a vast amount of persuading."

He offered up a weak smile and said, "Leave her to me. Putting myself in her shoes, I would feel the same." He left Sally and went to have a brief word with Lorne, then he addressed the room. "I have to go now, guys. Be good to my replacement. She's a reluctant participant, but I know you'll do the right thing and accept her as the boss's new partner, for now."

The rest of the team nodded, and Sally witnessed the relief cross Lorne's face.

"I'll see you soon. Be good and stay safe out there." With that, Jack was gone.

"Okay, whilst it's sad to see Jack leave us for a week or so, let's crack on with the cases we're working on," Sally said. "Jordan, will you be able to take up the slack on your case, without Lorne's assistance?"

"I'm sure I will, boss. All right if I run a few things past Lorne now, before she deserts me?" He grinned.

Lorne slapped a hand over her chest. "How to wound a girl with a cutting blow, Jordan Reid."

"Yes, that's fine," Sally said. "She's not going anywhere, you know, she'll still be around if you need expert guidance."

"Good to hear, thanks, boss."

"I'll give you half an hour to hand over the reins, Lorne, then we'll have a conflab in the office about the new case."

Lorne nodded and mock saluted her. Sally headed towards her office and collected her cup on the way. She sat behind her desk and, for a while, stared at the paperwork sitting in her in-tray and then picked up her mobile. She pushed a button and listened to the dial tone.

"Hello, you. This is unusual, you ringing me out of the blue. Is everything all right, Sal?" Simon asked.

"I needed to hear your voice. What are you up to?"

"Your dad and I are on our way to one of the sites. We're hoping to sign things off today and put it on the market. Depending how long the snagging list is."

"Ah, that sounds good. Are you on speaker?"

"Yes."

"Hi, Sally. Are you all right?" her father asked.

"I'll tell you guys later. Like I said, I was just checking in to see how things were going. An interesting case has come our way, and I met the new pathologist this morning at the scene."

"Oh? I hear she's keen to get on with things, is that right?" her husband asked.

"Yep, she seems very efficient. I think we're going to get on well together."

"Not like the grouch before her then." Simon laughed.

"He was good to work with, *occasionally*."

"Ha, bloody cheek. I'll get you for that later, Mrs Bracknall-Parker."

"Sorry, I couldn't resist. Have you got Dex with you?" At the sound of his name, her pooch barked. "Unless that was dad barking, I take it he's there," she added.

The three of them laughed. It felt good after the depressing start Sally had experienced to her day.

"I'll leave you to it," she said. "Will call you later, let you know what time I'll be home."

"Enjoy the rest of your day," Simon said.

Sally ended the call and attacked a few forms, vying for her attention on her desk until a knock on the door gave her the break she needed. "Come in."

Lorne stuck her head into the room. "Safe to enter now?"

"Nutter. Get your arse in here, partner."

Lorne cringed. "That's going to sound weird for a while. Hopefully, I won't have to be a stand-in for too long."

"You make it sound like it's going to be torture for you to be working closely alongside me. We've done it before when you were a DI. I know we were on a level playing field back then, but we got on great at the time, didn't we?"

"I know. But taking on this role was about me accepting less responsibility in my working life. I'm feeling oodles of pressure just talking about it."

"You're an idiot. No pressure from me, ever. The team needs you to step up, Lorne. No one else is qualified to handle this role, and DCI Green agreed with me, otherwise he wouldn't have suggested the temporary promotion. Christ, it's only going to be for a week or so. Is the thought of working with me closely again that unbearable?"

"Don't twist things. Of course it's not. I'm conscious of what the rest of the team are going to think, that's all."

"Don't be. They're not concerned, so why should you be? The decision is ultimately down to me whom I work alongside, and my better judgement placed you at the very top of the list."

"I'm grateful you have faith in me. I'll try not to let you down."

"I know you won't, you never have done in the past. Right, I'd better tell you what we're up against." Sally filled Lorne in on what she had discovered about the case so far, which didn't really amount to much. "What do you think? Where do you reckon we should go from here?"

"Are you testing me or is that a genuine question?"

"Give it a rest, Lorne. I'm aware of your capabilities."

"Okay. My first suggestion would be to work with the evidence you have to hand."

"The cloth and the belt buckle, is that what you're getting at?"

"Exactly. What about the remains themselves, do we know if the victim is male or female yet?"

"The pathologist believes we might be looking at a female victim but she still needs to corroborate it first. What would you do in my shoes?"

"With very little else to go on, I would be inclined to call a press conference. If you think the belt buckle is pretty distinctive, then I'd go with that first and foremost."

"It's a little rusty, we're going to have to put that on hold for the time being until SOCO get the chance to clean it up a bit. The last thing I want to do is sit here staring at the walls until they come back to me."

"You don't have to. All right, then the only other option on the table is to search through the missing persons files."

Sally pinched her chin between her finger and thumb. "How do we go about doing that?"

Lorne's nose creased. "First, we'd need to get a rough idea of how long the body has been in the water. When do you think the pathologist will likely be able to give us that information?"

"I'm not sure. Should I give her a call? I don't want her to think I'm hounding her at this early stage."

"Maybe leave it for now and give her a call first thing in the morning. Why don't I make a start by cobbling together a list of names of all those people who have been reported missing in the area in what, the last ten to fifteen years? Or should I go back further?"

Sally shrugged. "I'm at a loss. The person who dumped the body in the lake obviously knew what they were doing. Submerging a body in water can have devastating consequences on the body for so many different reasons. We don't know what state the corpse was in before it hit the water. I'm guessing it was more than likely to have been dismembered to have fitted into a single hessian sack. The next question would be, how long was the body kept before it was disposed of?"

Lorne sighed. "Too many variables and obvious questions for us to answer before the investigation has a chance to get underway."

Sally nodded. "We'll give both your suggestions a shot then, see what kind of results they produce for now. You delve into the missing person files, and I'll give Georgia a call, see if she can fit a press conference in, either this afternoon or tomorrow at the latest."

Lorne rose from her chair and then sucked in a breath. "Perhaps it would be wiser putting that on hold for a few days until the buckle has been cleaned up a little."

"Hmm… you're right. It won't do any harm sounding her out for now."

"Always good to have something in place rather than hang around for the waiting journos to play ball. Good luck."

"You, too. Do me a favour, check on Jordan if you get a chance, as well. His heart's in the right place, but his mind tends to wander now and again, without either me or Jack jumping up and down on his back."

"I'd rather not get that intimate with him, Tony would throttle me." Lorne winked and left the office.

Sally was left shaking her head. *I walked right into that one. Come back, Jack, all is forgiven.* She picked up the phone and rang the press department. "Georgia, it's DI Sally Parker, do you have a spare moment for a chat?"

"Sure. What's on your mind?"

Sally explained the situation and her dilemma about organising a press conference too soon.

"Ah yes, I can understand your apprehension. Why don't we book one for forty-eight hours from now? Maybe you can chase the lab up first thing and make them aware how imperative it is to have the belt buckle available for three p.m. on Thursday. How does that sound to you?"

"Ideal. I'd already made a note on my calendar to chase up the lab in the morning anyway. Any problems, let me know, Georgia, if you would?"

"If you'll do the same."

"That's an affirmative. If I don't see you about the station before Thursday, I'll see you at three, or just before."

"All the best until then, Inspector."

Sally ended the call and jotted down the details in her phone's calendar, something she was having to do more and more lately, with all that was going on in her life. When she wasn't at work, in the evening, Simon, even though he'd promised he wouldn't really involve her in his business, was always eager to discuss how his day had panned out and any interesting glitches that had arisen during the course of the day. Then he would ask her opinion on the mood boards he had thrown together on several properties nearing completion. She'd need to hold back from telling him to ask Lorne's opinion, after Lorne reminding her that she had also been involved in property developing once her marriage to her first husband had hit the rocks and she'd jacked in the force, either for the first or second time, Sally couldn't remember which.

Therefore, she really hadn't had that much of a chance to chill as such that often lately. Although, to escape Simon's enthusiastic attention to detail, her walks with Dex in the evening had recently been extended. Still, she counted herself lucky for having a caring husband who only wanted the best for her, unlike her first husband who was now rotting in prison.

She completed the rest of her paperwork and by the end of the day was mentally shattered. Before her shift ended, she sent a text to Jack to see how he was getting on. His brief response that he was fine and getting his head around things was what she needed to complete her day and put her mind at ease.

Sally passed on the message to the rest of the team and then sent them on their way for the evening. She followed Lorne home and flashed her farewell at the end of her road.

Dex greeted her with eagerness in the kitchen of the manor house they had bought in the last few years. Simon was in the kitchen, preparing their evening meal. She sniffed the air but failed to determine what was on the menu.

"What is it?" She hadn't had much of an appetite lately during the heatwave they had encountered; in truth, neither of them had. But for some reason, tonight she could eat a manky horse if it were put on the table in front of her.

"I'm trying something new. Why don't you take Dex for a walk? It'll be a while yet."

"Good idea. Come on, boy, let's go."

Sally slipped on the tatty trainers she preferred to use when exercising Dex and set off on an evening stroll around the neighbourhood.

The houses were few and far between in this neck of the woods. They were situated out in the countryside, which suited them. Not long into her stroll, she passed Lorne's house and waved at Tony who was crossing the driveway to fetch something from the garage.

"Pop in on your way back if you fancy a drink."

"I might do that, I'll see how it goes," she called over her shoulder. Dex gathered speed at the sight of another dog coming their way. "Calm down, Dex. Not every dog wants to become your friend."

The woman walking the large Rottweiler smiled and gripped the lead tightly. "He's not too clever with dogs he's never met before." With that, she stepped into the road, and they passed each other without either of the dogs kicking off.

Another five minutes, and they reached the idyllic walk down by the river. She unclipped Dex's lead and let him wander along the riverbank. The water level had dropped by over half, but it was still deep enough to allow a small leisure boat to sail past. Sally waved at the holidaymakers on board, and the female passenger waved back while the male concentrated on navigating the vessel around the bend up ahead.

She let Dex sniff the area for another ten minutes and then decided to head back home. Lorne was coming in the opposite direction with Sheba, her German Shepherd. Dex and Sheba were the best of friends so sniffed and played with each other during Sally and Lorne's brief chat.

"Everything all right? You seem a little subdued," Lorne asked.

"I'm fine. Deep in thought, wondering how Jack is coping and also working through the issues we have on the case so far."

"You really should learn to let things go once you get home, Sal. Mind you, I used to be exactly the same when I was a DI."

"Yeah, I know. I'll switch off once I'm at home. Dex is used to having me distracted when we're out and about. Any news on a new kennel manager yet?"

"Ah, yes. Tony interviewed a woman today. He reckons we should call her back for a second interview so that I can give her the once-over as well."

"Sounds positive. Does she have lots of experience?"

"That's the downside, not really, but Tony said Sheba took a liking to her."

"Half the job done then, eh? Dogs are great judges of character, so worth listening to."

"I guess. I'll ask if she can pop by and see me over the weekend."

"Right, I'd better be on my way. Simon was cooking up a storm in the kitchen when we left. He was eager for me to get out from under his feet."

"You don't know how lucky you are. All that training I've given Tony over the years, and I still get lumbered with knocking up dinner every night."

"Maybe you should add cooking skills to the kennel manager's duties and see where that leads you."

"Yeah, right. If I did that, I bet we'd still have a vacancy this time next year."

Sally laughed. "Probably. Have a good evening, see you in the morning."

"Enjoy your meal. I bet it'll be yummy as usual, not that I'm envious."

Fortunately, the meal was perfect. It consisted of roasted salmon in a creamy dill sauce with new potatoes, asparagus and baton carrots. All washed down with a classy white wine from Simon's collection, after which they retired to the lounge. Ten minutes later, Simon reached down beside the sofa and brought out the latest mood board he'd cobbled together for one of his newer renovation projects. Sally couldn't help but laugh at his childlike expression.

"Do we have time to go over some ideas I've put together?"

She shook her head. "As if I could possibly say no after you cooking me that delicious meal."

"It was all part of the plan." He winked and angled the

board more in her direction. "I'm going with a blue palette for this project, just to switch it around a little. What do you think?"

"This is for the Edwardian house you've converted into four flats, is it?"

"That's right. I've gone for the heritage tones throughout as the main colour but only using it on accent walls. I thought I'd pick up the colour with this mustard yellow in the curtains, blinds and cushions. What do you reckon?"

"You've nailed it. I think it's your best design yet and I can't wait to see the finished article."

He kissed her and beamed proudly at all his hard work.

"You love it, don't you? I mean the switch in careers."

He nodded. "Best move I've ever made, that is, apart from marrying you."

Sally leaned in for a kiss. "You're the best, Simon. I thank my lucky stars for having you in my life every morning when I wake up."

His cheeks flared to reflect the colour of the maroon cushion between them. "Teamwork. You're the perfect person to complement my life."

Sally smiled. "If you say so."

"Now that's my work out of the way, tell me how your day has been. What about this new case that you hinted at earlier?"

They spent the next hour or so discussing the ins and outs of the investigation so far. He offered up a few suggestions she could ask the new pathologist when the time came to speak with her again.

"Good ideas. Like I said earlier, she seems a decent enough woman."

"I'm glad they didn't bring in an old grouch, set in their ways."

"Me, too. Having just worked with someone of that ilk,

it's always a pleasure to have someone completely different to deal with."

"As you said such kind words about my mood board, I'm prepared to let that one slip… for now. Do you want a top-up?"

Sally held out her glass, and he filled it with the last of the wine.

"We can share this one," she said, "don't open another bottle at this time of night."

"Shall we call it a day and retire for the evening?"

"You read my mind. I'll just see to Dex first."

"I'll do that, you go ahead. I'll be up soon."

She leaned in for another kiss. "See, I knew I made the wisest move, marrying you."

## CHAPTER 2

It took a few days before the investigation really got underway. Sally had the belt buckle to hand ready for the conference, planned for that afternoon at three. The guys at the lab had done her proud, carried out all the necessary tests quicker than anticipated. She had received the call from the lab to say it was ready, so made a detour to pick up the buckle on the way into work that morning and was now taking a few minutes to examine it.

Lorne entered the room and stared at the glistening metal in the design of a Celtic knot. "It's beautiful. I can't imagine there are or were too many of those around at the time."

"That's what I'm thinking. Let's hope we get a flood of calls about it after I've held the conference this afternoon. Did you want to see me?" Sally asked, her eyes drawn to the manilla folder Lorne was holding flat against her torso.

Pauline had called by the office the previous day, something that was in itself unheard of, a pathologist going out of their way to pay the SIO on a case a personal visit. She had revealed the facts she had discovered about the remains so far. She believed, after speaking with a few of her pathologist colleagues, that the body had possibly been in the water for around five years, give or take a year either side. The corpse was a female, and she believed that the woman was possibly a mother, although she had stated that she was taking a punt on that front.

Sally had thanked Pauline and escorted her out of the building. The news, while it wasn't what you'd call extensive at this stage of the investigation, had come as a welcome contribution. Sally had passed the message on to Lorne, and she presumed that's why her new partner was standing in her office now, with the results of her research.

Lorne sat in the seat opposite and slid the folder across the desk.

Sally tilted her head and asked, "Anything of interest?"

"Five names. All of whom went missing around five years ago in the immediate area."

"Excellent. All women who had children?"

"Yes, that's correct. I've written down names and addresses of next of kin of all the women and verified with the electoral roll that the victims' families are mostly still at the residences, all except one."

"My, you have been busy. Let me have a sift through these and get back to you. Well done, Lorne. Do you want to join me this afternoon for the conference or would you rather keep out of the limelight nowadays?"

"I'd love to join you, but my crow's feet are telling me to be cautious."

Sally shook her head and laughed. "You're nuts. You still have beautiful skin, you don't look a day over…" She paused.

Lorne wagged a finger. "Don't even go there."

"I was about to say you don't look a day over forty, but you'd probably call me a liar."

"Too right I would, and no, I have no intention of revealing the truth."

"It's okay, I only have to bring up your personnel file to find out your real age."

"Drat. Okay, you win. Anyway, no, I'd rather sit this one out."

"Fine by me. We have an hour to wait before the journalists show up. The conference should take another hour, tops. That'll leave us an hour or so before we call it a day. Might be worth dropping by the first next of kin, then, what do you reckon?"

"I could have a flick through them, see if there are any on the way home, and we could kill two birds with one stone, if you like?"

"Sounds like the perfect scenario to me."

"Leave it with me. I just wanted to give you a bit of encouraging news before you go down there and get ripped apart."

Sally cringed. "Ouch, I hope that isn't the outcome of today's conference. I could do without the added stress."

"Sorry, I was only teasing. Anything I can do to help with the preparations?"

"No, I'm all sorted, I think."

Lorne left the office, taking the folder with her. Sally scribbled down some notes that she was hoping to bring up during her time on camera. However, her main priority would be to focus on the belt buckle.

*Someone, somewhere must recognise it, they have to. Although, I have a niggling feeling in my gut that simply isn't going to be the case.*

SALLY MET up with Georgia in the hallway outside the designated press conference room. Her stomach matched the knot on the belt buckle. She hated holding meetings with the press. She'd had her fair share of run-ins with some of the journalists over the years, so much so that it had unnerved her when she'd conducted the last few.

Georgia ran a hand up and down Sally's arm. "Take a deep breath, hold it for a few seconds, and then let it out. You're worrying unnecessarily. Any sign of trouble, I'll draw the meeting to a halt, have faith. You know they're going to sense your anguish, so my advice would be not to give them the ammunition in the first place."

Sally nodded and held in the breath she'd been advised to suck in. Letting it out, she said, "You always know how to calm me down. Does holding these conferences have this effect on other officers, or am I the only one who gets freaked out by them?"

Georgia scratched her head. "I've known a couple of officers throw up in the loo before now, so you're definitely not alone."

"Heck. I'm glad I'm not that bad. All right, let's get this over and done with."

"That's the spirit. Smile; in my experience it helps to disguise the nerves."

Sally fixed a half-smile in place, not wishing to come across as a complete idiot, lacking in compassion, and took a step into the room which instantly fell silent.

Georgia introduced Sally and the reason they were there, and then Sally took over. Thanks to Georgia's superb coaching, she breezed through the conference until it came to the journalists bombarding her with questions.

"Who would dump a body in the lake like that?"

"How long has it been in there?"

"Would it have remained undiscovered if the drought hadn't occurred?"

"What leads do you have about the deceased, apart from the belt buckle?"

Most of the questions Sally went down the politician

route of answering, by avoiding them as much as possible, but a couple of the journalists kept badgering, repeating the same question over and over. In the end, she was forced to give them what they wanted, or close to it. Some of them accepted her answers, but others did their best to unnerve her and coerce her into making a mistake and giving too much information away. That's when Georgia came to her rescue and drew the conference to a halt. Much to Sally's relief.

Outside in the hallway and, out of sight of the journos, she blew out the breath she'd been holding in. "Damn, I hate them."

"Sadly, they're a necessary evil. I have to say, I thought you got off lightly today."

"I'll have to take your word on that one. Thanks, Georgia, for making sure I kept my cool and for reining them in when they got out of hand."

"My pleasure. I hope something good comes of it. That's the aim, after all."

"It sure is. We live in hope. Speak soon."

Sally went back upstairs and eased into the room which was a hive of activity. Lorne was sitting next to Jordan, going over some issues he had regarding the case Lorne had already been working on before Sally had pulled her off it.

"Everything all right?" Sally asked on her way to pour herself a coffee.

"Jordan has suggested he goes out to the prison to visit Billy Prather. We're running through the reasons why we shouldn't do that just yet."

"Remind me about the case?" Sally asked. She stopped next to Jordan's desk and blew on her piping-hot drink.

Lorne gestured for Jordan to fill Sally in. "He's always protested his innocence, told the court that the evidence the police had put in front of them had been planted."

"I see. What sort of evidence?"

"Billy told the police that when his girlfriend, Christine Newman, went missing she was wearing a pair of white trainers with a blue stripe. DI Falkirk searched the premises and found a pair of trainers shoved at the back of the wardrobe, or so he said."

"Maybe she had two pairs the same, it's not unheard of," Sally suggested.

Jordan grunted. "Christine was a size five, and the trainers Falkirk found, or planted, were a size four."

"Ouch, had it been the other way round, a size larger, then I might have been willing to accept it, but not a size smaller. Jesus, and that resulted in Prather's conviction?"

"Yep. Hard to believe. There were other snippets of evidence like Prather not having a viable alibi for around the time she went missing, but that was the damning piece of the puzzle that led to his arrest and resulted in him being banged up for fifteen years."

"On a murder charge? Without a damn body? Hard to fathom that a jury could be coerced into thinking he was guilty and put him away. Falkirk must have been a law unto himself and had that many people in his pocket…"

"Right, makes you wonder how far his influence reached, doesn't it?" Lorne added.

"Okay, I've heard enough. Visit Prather, take the file with you, go over his statement and why he believes he was stitched up. Also, ask him to try and give us another lead to go on, anything to help us with the investigation. Do you want to take someone with you?"

Jordan waved away the suggestion. "I'm fine, boss. I'll call the prison now, see if I can set up an appointment."

"Try and get in to see him before the weekend, Jordan. Keep me informed."

"I'll do my best."

Lorne patted the young officer on the shoulder, rose from her seat and returned to her desk.

Sally shifted to stand alongside Lorne.

"How did it go?" Lorne asked.

"All right, I guess. I think they got a waft of my fear, but only a few of them chose to hound me more than was necessary. All we have to do now is man the phones in the hope that someone will recognise that belt buckle and the bits of cloth."

"What are the odds on the family seeing the news bulletin? If it's been years since the victim was reported missing."

"One of those occasions when we need to remain positive." Sally inched towards her office. "I have a few mundane tasks to perform, and then we'll set off. Give me thirty minutes or so."

"I'll be ready and waiting."

TRUE TO HER WORD, Sally emerged from her office in the time she had stated. After bidding the rest of the team farewell and instructing them to leave at five-thirty, Sally and Lorne left the station. They decided it would be best to leave Lorne's car there overnight.

"So, who are we due to see first?" Sally asked.

"The closest one which is on our way home is Eve Porter. She went missing five years ago. Her husband, Gary, found her car empty by the side of the road; she was nowhere to be seen. But it was her mother, Jocelyn, who rang the police."

"And not the husband? How come?"

"Apparently, Jocelyn Wyatt was furious and pointed the finger at the husband."

Sally briefly turned to face Lorne and asked, "Any particular reason?" She faced the road again and then drew to a stop at a red light.

"It came out later that Gary had been having an affair at the time."

Sally lashed out at the steering wheel. "What is bloody wrong with men? No, don't answer that, we'll be discussing that topic non-stop for decades without coming to a conclusion."

Lorne laughed. "So true. Best to be avoided at all costs."

The traffic flowed once more. "We're nearly there now. Have you managed to find out anything else about the husband?"

"Not as such. On the electoral roll I noticed there's another woman living at the house now, who goes under the name of Anna Clarke, which would suggest he has another significant other."

"Interesting. Okay, we'll see how this pans out. We're close now. Another left and right, and that's us. You called ahead and made sure he was in, didn't you?"

"Of course. He's working nights this week, not due to start until seven, so he said he'd be willing to hang around and speak with us."

"Could you gauge his reaction when you requested a meeting?"

"He seemed fine, maybe a little put out, but otherwise okay."

"We'll find out soon enough. Did Falkirk interview him the first time around, or was he under the spotlight with another inspector?"

"No, it was Falkirk."

"Ah, right. That's sounding alarm bells, something to be aware of. We'll go in all smiles, try to get him onside first and go from there."

"I was about to suggest the same. Will you mention the belt buckle? I doubt if the news conference has aired yet."

"Yes, I've got a photo of it on my phone. I'll mention it, see what type of reaction we get from him. Here it is now, fifty-eight, is that right?"

"Correct. Seems a bit run-down."

Sally cast her eye over the other houses in the terrace. "Keeping up with the neighbours in that respect, there's not a decent one amongst them. Not that I'm one to judge."

Lorne grinned at her. "If you say so."

"Brace yourself for a backlash. I'll be shocked if we don't receive one."

"Maybe we should have signed out a couple of Tasers in that case."

"Christ, don't even joke about it. Ready?"

"Yep, I'll be right behind you."

Sally rubbed at her chin. "Not the answer Jack would have given me. He would have offered to be the first in line."

"Shame he's not here then." Lorne grinned again.

They left the vehicle, and with the rough neighbourhood in mind, Sally made sure she locked it and set the alarm. She rang the bell. The row of houses lacked front gardens, and there was no sign of hanging baskets to brighten the road.

*They'd probably get smashed up within days, anyway.*

A man in his early forties, with a slight beard, opened the door. Sally and Lorne produced their IDs.

"Mr Porter?" Sally asked.

He nodded.

"I'm DI Sally Parker, and this is my partner, DS Lorne Warner. We contacted you earlier."

"That's right. What's this about?"

"It would be better if we spoke inside, sir."

He gave a shrug and walked ahead up the cluttered hallway. "Don't mind the mess, it comes with having kids who are spoilt, who have too many toys to their name."

Sally ignored all the bikes stacked up against the wall and walked sideways up the narrow space to what was meant to be the lounge which was equally messy with toys strewn across the floor and every surface.

"Told you. And don't think I don't give this place a tidy now and again, you know what kids are like."

Sally glanced at Lorne who avoided eye contact with her. "Don't worry, we're not here to judge."

"Makes a change. You lot usually do."

Sally searched the room for an appropriate seat to use. Porter took the hint and cleared two places on the sofa. Sally lowered herself but remained on the edge of the worn, food-encrusted leather sofa. Lorne did exactly the same beside her.

Porter returned to the only other clear seat, the armchair closest to the fireplace alongside a gas fire which had seen better days. Sally couldn't help wondering if it had received a safety check in the last few years. She doubted it.

"Come on then. On the phone you mentioned this had something to do with my wife going missing. Don't tell me she's turned up after all these years?"

"We're not sure. It's true, we've discovered some human remains."

He gasped and shook his head.

"But we have no way of identifying the corpse yet."

"What's that supposed to mean? I don't understand what you're saying."

"We believe the body has been in water for at least five years. Our aim is to visit the families of all those who were reported missing around that time, hence the reason we got in touch with you today."

He gave her a blank look and shrugged. "That doesn't

make sense. If you can't identify the body… hang on, do you know what sex it is? Sorry, gender, that's what you call it, isn't it?"

"That's right. Yes, we know the remains are that of a female. Would you mind running through what happened when you reported your wife missing?"

"I didn't. That bitch of a mother-in-law reported it before I got the chance to, and that's when it all kicked off."

Sally inclined her head. "Can you fill us in on the details, if it's not too painful for you?"

"I got over having any feelings about the case years ago. She did a runner and landed me in a lot of bother. Your lot had no right treating me like a frigging criminal. That bastard, Falkirk, he arrested me for killing her. How he got away with that I'll never know. Aren't you supposed to have a body show up before you start pointing the finger at someone?"

"Not necessarily. Did you give him any cause to think you were guilty?"

"Not that I can think of. But the ex-mother-in-law had plenty to say about it. More fool him for listening to her poisonous tongue."

"Can you tell us what happened? The reason I'm asking is that our Cold Case Team was set up a few years ago with specific instructions to delve into DI Falkirk's cases."

He raised a finger and seethed. "I knew that tosser was bent, you could tell."

"I can only apologise for what he put you through at the time."

"Despicable, it was. He had a way of making you feel guilty even if you'd never put a foot wrong in life before. Scumbag, that's what he was."

"I can't argue with that. We've been dealing with some dreadful cases, you're one of the fortunate ones."

"Ha, you're having a laugh, aren't you? The way that moron treated me."

"Some people have been in prison for years. We've freed them but we can never make up for the injustice they've suffered over the years."

"*If* they survived. Don't tell me a few of them haven't ended their lives?"

Sally sighed. "Sadly, yes, that's true. Was there anything about your situation that would have caused Falkirk to have been suspicious?"

His gaze dropped to his clenched hands. "Yes, I can't deny it, thinking back, although I was fuming at the time."

"And that was?"

"I was having an affair," he said without hesitation. "My marriage wasn't a happy one. We had two young kids at the time who drove me nuts." He cast an eye around the room. "They still do. But, just because we were unhappy, it doesn't mean that I would go out and kill her. I still reckon she did a runner. I wouldn't have put it past her to have had a bit on the side as well."

"And this is the first time the police have been in touch since?"

"Meaning?"

"There has been no sign of your wife since she disappeared?"

"Not that I know of. You'd be better off asking her mother that question."

"You haven't spoken to her since?"

"I try not to. She has rights regarding the children. I never stop her seeing them, but if she tried anything on, like keeping them longer than the stipulated time, there would be hell to pay."

"And she's never mentioned Eve to you?"

"Nope. I don't want to know. She left me bringing up the

kids. It might not look like it, but Anna and I have done our best to give them a good home. They want for nothing, you can see that."

"I can tell. Do you have your mother-in-law's address?"

"Yeah, somewhere. I'll have to find my phone." He got up and hunted for it. "Damn thing, where is it? Shit! Sorry, it's in the kitchen, I won't be a tick."

He marched out of the room and returned within a few seconds with a slim redhead. "This is Anna, my partner. All right if she sits in on this?"

"Hi, I'm DI Parker, and this is DS Warner. Feel free to join us."

"Thanks. Gary briefly filled me in. So, you've found a body. Do you know if it's her or not?"

"It's impossible to tell at this stage. We have five possible leads. If they don't bear any fruit then we're up the creek. Have you two been together long?"

The couple appeared shifty, and Sally soon realised that Anna must have been the one Gary was having an affair with at the time his wife went missing. "Ah, you were together when Eve went missing, is that correct?"

Anna held up her hands. "Guilty as charged. The marriage was in dire straits anyway, it's not like I came along and unsteadied the ship. It was on the verge of sinking long before I showed up."

"That's true," Gary said. "Ah, here it is. Who wants it?"

Lorne held out her hand to take the mobile from Gary and jotted down the relevant details in her notebook before giving it back to him.

Anna sat on the arm of the chair next to Gary. "Where was the body found?"

"At Cavendish Lake. It's dried up due to the drought. If it hadn't, I doubt the remains would have been found."

"And they've been there around five years, is that what the assumption is?" Anna asked.

"We have no way of knowing that. There is one thing... actually, several things I'd like to run past you, if it's okay?" Sally directed her question at Gary.

"Go on. I'll help if I can."

Sally removed her phone from her jacket pocket and scrolled to the latest photo. She showed him the belt buckle. "Do you recognise this?"

He took the phone and studied the photo from different angles. "Nope, should I?"

"It was found at the bottom of the sack in which the remains were discovered."

"I see. What is it?"

Sally scrolled to the next photo. "It's a belt buckle. What about these pieces of cloth, do they seem familiar at all?"

He stared at the photos for a few seconds then shook his head and passed the phone back to her. "No, they don't, should they?"

"Again, these were remnants of fabric unearthed at the scene this morning."

"I can't help you. What happens next? Can't you match any DNA?"

"There are ways, but it's going to take time to get the results. That's why we've taken a risk and decided to visit the families of those who were reported missing around five years ago. Hopefully, it won't cause the families too much distress, dredging up the past."

"It hasn't. Well, maybe a little. I'm bitter about what happened for several reasons; firstly because of the way that *wanker* treated me and, secondly because I still think Eve took off, even though her mother has always denied knowing anything. Maybe if you guys hound her enough, she'll fold and reveal the truth."

"I have to ask, what kind of mother was Eve?"

"She was all right. She suffered from post-natal depression after both births and refused to let me near her in bed after the second one was born. That's why the marriage was failing."

"Understandable. Did she try to seek help for her problem?"

"No. She denied she had one."

"Would she simply run off and leave her kids behind?" Sally queried.

"Who knows? She was depressed, anything and everything could have been going on in that head of hers," Gary admitted.

"When you hand your kids over to your mother-in-law, do you think she might be taking them to see her daughter?"

"I can't say it hasn't crossed my mind. I'll be livid if that is the case because that means they've been forcing my kids to lie to me. Can't stand the thought of them doing that, it's not right, is it?"

"Maybe it is pure speculation on my part, in that case. I have a suspicious mind, every copper has." Sally smiled.

"I can believe it. Is there anything else you want from us today?"

A large bang happened overhead.

Anna leapt to her feet and went to investigate. "What's going on up here? What have we told you about jumping up and down on that bed?"

"Same old thing," Gary said. "They've got all these toys, they play with them for a few minutes when they get home from school, and that's it, off to their bedroom they go until their dinner appears on the table. Drive me bloody potty, they do, but I love the bones of them, so what can I do about it?"

"Sounds like they run you both ragged at times." Sally smiled.

"Mostly that's true, however, their resilience never ceases to amaze me. They took to Anna really well when she moved in." He leaned forward and lowered his voice. "I wouldn't go shouting too loud about it because she'll likely get a fat head, but she's been more of a mother to those kids than Eve ever was."

"Maybe her illness prevented her from forming any kind of maternal bond with the children."

He hitched up a shoulder and inhaled a breath that inflated his chest. "Perhaps, who knows? What happens now?"

"We're going to pay Jocelyn a visit, see what she has to say about the situation."

"No, I meant with regard to the body."

"It's a waiting game. The lab is carrying out dozens of in-depth tests to find the DNA needed to make a formal identification. Which, in all honesty, could take a few days to materialise. It won't stop us continuing with the investigation, from contacting the other families. If nothing comes from that, then we'll dig deeper and harder until we make a connection and give the family concerned the closure they need to get on with their lives."

"Yeah, that would be nice, something we all strive for, not that I haven't, you know, being with Anna. It's the kids I feel sorry for… What if she suddenly drifted back into their lives, what then? You can't mess with their state of mind, it's not fair, is it?"

"It's not. Let's see what Jocelyn has to say and go from there."

"Will you let me know?"

"If anything important comes from our questioning,

you'll be the first to be told. Thanks for agreeing to see us. We'll leave you to enjoy the rest of your evening."

"Get ready for work, you mean. I get paid more money for working nights. It's a necessity at the moment. I should have said, Anna is pregnant."

Sally beamed. "That's wonderful news. You must both be delighted."

"We are, in our own way. She's been wanting a kid of her own for a few years. I finally caved in, and she fell pregnant right away. I'll pass on your congratulations." He showed them back up the hallway to the front door.

"Please do. Take care of each other, Gary. Sorry we couldn't bring you better news."

"Like I said, I've got an inkling her body will never be found because she's still alive."

"We're going to do all we can to discover the truth. Hopefully, visiting Jocelyn will put us on the right path."

"Good luck, she's always been a secretive cow."

JOCELYN'S HOUSE was a fifteen-minute drive from Gary's. They were only a few streets away now.

"We might as well fit this visit in tonight and then we can move on to another family in the morning," Sally said.

"Just so I can get my head around this, we're here because of what Gary told us and not because we believe the remains we discovered are her daughter's, right?"

"Bingo. I believe him, don't you? And if this woman is hiding something, I intend to find out what it is."

"As you do," Lorne replied.

"Here we are now. Hopefully, we'll be in and out in no time at all."

"Let's wait and see, shall we?"

Sally smiled and stepped out of the car. The semi-detached house was situated in a much cleaner and generally better estate than Gary's, therefore, Sally felt more at ease as she walked up the concrete path and rang the bell. She turned back to admire the well-laid-out garden which, by the look of things, was tended to regularly by the homeowner. "Nice display. Wish I had the time to do something with our back garden. Simon keeps suggesting getting in a landscaper, but you have to give them an idea of what you want, and that's what is flummoxing me. Neither of us is what you'd call green-fingered, and I wouldn't have a clue where to blooming start."

"I used to like pottering around in the garden years ago, on one of my many breaks from the force. If you want to go down that route, I think I have some gardening books lying around that I can dig out for you. I could even give you a hand with putting a few ideas down on paper. No pressure, when we're less busy, of course."

"You would? That'd be cool. I definitely need an expert hand to guide me."

"I'm no expert, let's not get carried away now."

Sally bared her teeth. "You are, compared to me. Come on, back to work, I'm dying to find out what this woman is hiding, if anything."

"Me, too. She's taking an eternity to answer the bell. Want me to check around the back, see if she's around there?"

Just then, the front door opened, and a woman in her sixties, maybe early seventies, wearing an apron covered in flour, eyed them warily. "Sorry, I was baking in the kitchen. Can I help?"

Sally and Lorne flashed their IDs. "DI Sally Parker and DS Lorne Warner. Do you have a spare moment, Mrs Wyatt?"

She wiped her hands on her apron, seemingly flustered to have the police standing on the doorstep, unless that was in

Sally's mind. "Oh, the police. What's this about? Have I done something wrong?"

"No, not at all. Would it be possible for us to come in for a quick chat? I appreciate what time it is, but we were in the area and thought we'd drop in on our way home from work."

"Of course." Jocelyn took a few steps back into the large clutter-free hallway and again wiped her hands on her apron. "Would you like a drink?"

"No, we're fine. Thanks for the offer, though."

She cast a swift glance up the stairs and then turned to enter the first room on the right. "You'd better come into the lounge. Excuse the mess. Baking takes priority in this house, I've been at it most of the day." She lowered herself into one of the two small sofas and gestured for Sally and Lorne to join her.

"We won't keep you from your baking long, I promise. Do you live alone?"

Jocelyn crossed her legs at the ankles and stared down at her feet. "Yes, that's right. Ah, I have a feeling I know what's coming next: why am I slaving in the kitchen if I only have myself to fend for?"

Sally shrugged. "It's not something that would appeal to me, but cooking has always been a chore, in my opinion. I tend to do it out of necessity not because I want to."

"I'm the same," Lorne added to the conversation.

"I'm not surprised, you must be super busy ladies, whereas I'm retired and have plenty of spare time to fill. I have a coffee morning I need to prepare for tomorrow. I'm a member of the Women's Institute, and we're trying to raise a hundred thousand by Christmas to help struggling families in the local area get through the cost-of-living crisis."

"That's admirable of you."

"We do what we can. I try to help others out as much as I can, it helps me come to terms with the loss of my daughter."

"I see. I hope it helps."

"Sometimes. It distracts me for a while, keeping my hands busy. I don't have the time or mental energy to sit and relive the tragic events. I take it this has something to do with what happened to her?" She wiped her clean hands on her apron yet again and sat back.

"Yes, actually it does. There will be a news bulletin going out this evening, revealing that the remains of a corpse have been found."

Jocelyn's hands slapped against her cheeks, and she gasped. "No. And you think…?"

"It's a possibility, although having just come from seeing Gary, we're unsure if we're on the right lines."

"I don't understand."

Sally withdrew her phone from her pocket and showed it to Jocelyn. "This was in the bag along with the remains. Do you recognise it?"

Jocelyn's gaze dropped to the phone, and a frown pinched her forehead. "I don't think so, is it a buckle?"

"Yes, a belt buckle."

"No, although I can't be sure. I don't think Eve ever wore a belt."

"That's exactly the type of information we wanted to hear. After looking over the notes from the case, it came to our attention that it was you who contacted the police about your daughter's disappearance, is that correct?"

"Yes. I had to. I couldn't leave it up to that lazy bastard to do it. Excuse my language. You say you've just been to see him, then you'll know what I mean, if he let you into the house."

"He did."

"Those children, my beautiful grandchildren, shouldn't be subjected to living in a hovel like that. I've tried several times over the years to get custody of them, but it's such a struggle dealing with the law when you're on your own."

"I can imagine. Forgive me for asking, but do you really think it would be a good idea having the kids living here with you at your time of life?" Sally cringed as the words poured out of her mouth before she had a chance to stop them.

"I'm sixty-eight, not eighty-eight. Yes, I might have slowed down the last few years but I have time on my hands to put their needs first. Look around you and tell me where you think they'd be better off?"

There was no denying the woman was right, but in Sally's opinion, the children still belonged with their last remaining parent, not living with a grandparent. "I don't have a clue about raising children as I've never had any of my own, but I would think it's down to having a good relationship with them rather than how tidy the house is."

Jocelyn glared at her through narrowed eyes. "If you say so. I haven't seen the state their bedrooms are in, of course, but if the downstairs is anything to go by, how is that seen as good parenting with dozens of trip hazards lying around? They've got a garden shed, he could put the damn bikes and toys that are for external use out there, couldn't he? Except he's too lazy. And now I hear that there's another one on the way… unbelievable!"

"The children told you the news?"

"Yes, they never keep anything from me. They're not happy there. Why do you think I've constantly fought the system over the years… only to get nowhere? It breaks my heart having to hand them back after they've spent the weekend with me. They're so relaxed when they're here. I assure you, having a tidy house means a lot to children as well, even though some adults might presume otherwise. You could eat off the floor here, not that you'd want to, something you wouldn't be able to do round at Gary's. That's what I'm getting at. You know what kids are like about dropping their food and picking it up and popping it in their mouths. Can you imagine what those children are ingesting with that filth lying around?"

Sally nodded. "Fair point. If we can recap what happened with your daughter, what, five years ago?"

"That's right, although it feels more like ten. I still expect her to walk through the door any moment. I cry myself to sleep most nights. She was my only child, and I miss her terribly."

"At the time, you thought Gary had harmed your daughter, is that right?"

"No, I thought he'd *killed* her. Nothing has changed over the years. I've detested having to deal with him but there was no way I could have given up on my grandchildren, they're all I have left of Eve. I see her in both of them. They have the same eye colour, the same smile, the same mannerisms as she had."

"Do you still believe he is behind your daughter's disappearance?"

"Yes. Don't you? You've already told me you read the file. He was having an affair with that woman, and then one day my daughter goes missing. You don't have to be a genius to work it out, or do you?"

"There is such a thing as coincidence. Did your daughter ever discuss their marriage with you?"

"All the time. She was saving up, trying to get some money behind her to pluck up the courage to leave him."

"We've been told that she was suffering from post-natal depression. Was she?"

"Initially, after the children were born, but that wore off after six months or so. I think Gary has always clung on to the issue and used it as an excuse when discussing her whereabouts."

Sally nodded and sucked in a breath. "I'm going to lay my cards on the table here and tell you what his theory is."

Jocelyn sat forward again. "I'm listening. Surprise me."

"He believes that Eve is alive and that you know where she is."

Jocelyn laughed and tipped back in her seat again. "And you *believe* him?"

Sally cast an eye around the room and spotted a picture frame on the mantelpiece. Ignoring Jocelyn's question, she asked, "Is that Eve?"

"Yes, that's her. My one and only beautiful daughter. That was taken when she was expecting Darcy, her first child. She was radiant throughout the pregnancy, but to see her a few days after, her emotions going into a downward spiral, it was heartbreaking beyond words, I can tell you."

"I can imagine. And since her disappearance you've had no form of contact with her, either via a letter or a phone call when there was no one on the other end of the line? Anything like that?"

"Nothing. I would have got to the truth. Hunted her down and brought her home rather than have to deal with the torment of not knowing whether she is dead or alive."

"Is there a special place she liked to visit?"

"Don't think I haven't tried them all. I've visited various locations over the years, from Cornwall up to the Lakes to where she classed as her special places, and nothing. Trust me, if she was still alive, I would have found her by now and dragged her back home where she belongs, here with me, rather than go through all this uncertainty that I have to live with day in and day out."

"I think I would feel the same. I don't envy you or the

situation you find yourself in. I hope you discover the closure you need one day soon."

"Me, too. I lie in bed and pray that she will walk back into my life again. I try not to think about the alternative. I hope the family of the deceased find some peace soon."

"I'm sure they will. Take care of yourself."

Sally and Lorne rose from their seats and followed Jocelyn to the front door, her eyes drawn to the stairs, and Sally turned to see what she was looking at, but there was no one there. She suppressed a shudder before they left the house.

"What did you make of her?" Sally asked Lorne.

Lorne waited until they were back in the car before she replied, "Out of the two of them, I'm inclined to come down on Gary's side. What's your take on it?"

"I believe there was someone else in the house." Sally quickly dipped and looked at the upstairs window. An outline of a figure jumped back.

"I got that impression, too. Unless…"

"Unless?"

"It was the spirit of her dead daughter."

"I had to hold back a shudder in the hallway on the way out. Maybe we should contact your friend down in London?"

"Carol? There's no need. She's on her way up here for the weekend. I've finally persuaded her to come and stay with us."

"Why? After all this time?"

"She has always had reservations about staying with anyone else, not just me and Tony."

Sally started the engine. "Any specific reason?"

"She's afraid of unsettling her visitors."

Sally frowned and faced Lorne. "Visitors?"

"The spirits who act as her guides. If she remains in the same house then that suits all of them, including her."

"So, why has she changed her mind?"

"My nagging is probably the cause of that and the fact she hates being alone in the house now since the fella she was involved with has passed over."

"Wait, doesn't he still visit her? Or rather, his spirit?"

"No. She told him not to."

Sally roared with laughter. "Oh my, is that a possibility? To pick and choose who visits you in the afterlife?"

"Apparently. Anyway, she'll be arriving Friday, and I can't wait to see her. I just wish Charlie was coming with her. The trouble is, she and Katy are working a huge case, down there in the Big Smoke, that is taking up all of her spare time."

"She's a credit to you, Lorne. Becoming a sergeant at such a young age. I'm glad Katy pushed her to sit the exam. I can see her going far in the Met. God knows they're in dire need of turning things around down there after the bad reputation they've acquired in the last few years."

"Tell me about it. Although both Katy and Charlie have told me they've considered throwing in the towel lately."

"Did they mention why?"

"Because of the flack they've received from the general public. As if their job wasn't hard enough before, it's gone up tenfold since that bastard of an officer got sent down for killing that woman. I bet Pete was turning in his grave when he heard about that."

"You still miss him, after all these years, don't you?" Sally asked quietly.

Lorne sniffled. "Don't... he's never really far from my thoughts. That was the hardest part about leaving London, giving up on his presence around me."

Sally's shoulders wiggled. "Don't say that. I have chills running up my spine now. I hate to ask, but didn't his spirit come with you?"

"No, I've never felt him around me up here. Maybe he

decided to stay there and watch over Charlie for me. He adored her when she was younger."

"Perhaps you're right. Ask Carol when she comes up, see if that's a possibility."

"I might just do that. Want me to mention our case to her over the weekend, if we haven't solved it by then?"

"I doubt if that will happen with no clues at our disposal, except for the belt buckle. Why not, do you think she'll mind?"

"I'll let her settle in first and then ask her on Sunday, how's that?"

"The perfect conversation over a nice roast dinner."

They both laughed.

## CHAPTER 3

Sally beeped her horn and picked Lorne up at eight-thirty the following morning. "How did you sleep last night?"

"Apart from it being really sticky, despite having the windows open, I slept okay on and off. How about you?" Lorne asked.

"I had the case going round and round in my head, or more to the point, what we encountered yesterday with Gary and Jocelyn. One of them isn't telling the truth, however, neither of them recognised the one piece of evidence that we're hoping will help to identify the remains."

"True enough. In other words, you don't think we should dwell on it but think we should move on to the next family."

"You took the words out of my mouth. Let's face it, every family has its secrets. Christ, remember that case we solved together? That must have been five or six years ago now, the matriarch of the family was a law unto herself. The lies and deception surrounding that family was like nothing else I've ever experienced before… and never want to again, anytime soon."

"I wonder how she's survived in prison all these years."

"Might be interesting to check it out, when we get a spare half an hour or so."

"I'll do it, once we've finished with this case. You've got me intrigued now. I wouldn't put it past her to be running the prison by now. She was such a manipulative bitch, wasn't she?"

"Claire Knight, that was her name, wasn't it? Makes my skin crawl thinking about her and the crimes she committed. But, come the end, we cottoned on to the games she was playing and the jury helped to put her behind bars where she belongs."

"That's right. How could I ever forget that name? I don't think I've ever felt more satisfied as a copper dealing with that bitch."

Sally faced her again. "You might want to revisit that answer."

Lorne gave her a puzzled look. "I'm not with you."

"The Unicorn and his demise."

Lorne raised a finger. "Ah, yes, no, that was after I left the force. You remember, Tony came knocking on my door seeking my help and pleaded with me to travel to France."

"That's right. It had slipped my mind. God, you've had some adventures over the years, haven't you?"

"More than any other female Inspector I know, present company excepted."

"No, you win hands down. What's your biggest regret in life?"

"Personally or professionally?"

"Either. Maybe they're even linked. Go for it."

"Apart from marrying Tom, my biggest regret is not being able to save Pete's life."

"Oh, Lorne. Knowing you the way I do, I'm sure you did your very best. I believe when our time is up, there's little you or anyone else can do to prevent the inevitable from happening."

Lorne sighed and wiped her eyes with her sleeve. "I know. But it still eats away at me. That bastard, the Unicorn, cut me off from Pete, he was out of my reach. I gave him mouth-to-mouth, he would have relished that but, in the end, he faded away before my eyes."

"Bless you. You did your best. The shots were still raining down on you in that alley, there was nothing else you could have done, except risk your own life."

"But the Unicorn wanted me alive. I didn't realise that at the time, otherwise I would have dodged the bullets to have got to him."

"What an absolute arsehole he was. I'm glad you had the satisfaction of taking him down yourself, after what he put you and your family through."

"Charlie is still carrying the scars, physically and mentally. That's yet another regret I have, putting her in danger."

"It's the risk we take, signing up to become coppers, isn't it? I know it's not fair putting our families at risk, but there is so much satisfaction to be gained when we solve an investigation and get the filthy scum off our streets."

"Only for them to be replaced by worse criminals many times over. Anyway, enough about me, what's your biggest regret?"

"You know what I'm going to say. Being duped by that bastard of an ex-husband of mine. Smarmy effing shit."

Lorne placed a hand on Sally's arm. "You came through it. I know it took you a few years to get over him, but if you hadn't, you and Simon wouldn't be married. There's always a positive to cling to, love."

"I suppose. He's an amazing man. It still remains to be

seen whether he's done the right thing giving up the career he trained so hard for, though."

"Get away with you, he's knocking it out of the park being a property developer. Tony often tells me he's in awe of his negotiating skills, whether that involves going after a good deal for materials or standing his ground when dealing with agents."

"I'm glad he has Tony alongside him. Fancy that, eh? Those two working together, with Dad chipping in now and again, and the two of us standing side by side. All right, if it hadn't been for Jack needing to take an enforced break, we wouldn't be in this situation now, but let's make the most of it and show the others how it's done, eh, kiddo?"

Lorne raised her thumb. "I'm up for it, if you are. I don't suppose you've heard from Jack, have you?"

"He rang me last night, just a quick call. Poor bloke sounded so downhearted, I couldn't think of anything decent to say to him. Of course, I offered him my deepest sympathy when he told me what had happened. But I felt lost, unable to function properly. I don't think I've ever felt that way before, not when dealing with someone's grief."

"Don't be too hard on yourself. Being nosey, did he tell you how the accident occurred?"

"They're not sure. They've found some CCTV footage of the accident and they're doing their utmost to pick it to pieces. I think the upshot is that another car ploughed into him while he was pulling away from the lights."

"Sounds like the other car jumped a red light."

"Possibly. Again, I wouldn't like to speculate. What a way to go. His father was a fit man, just celebrated his sixty-eighth birthday only last week."

"Poor Jack, his children must be distraught as well."

"They all are. Life can be grossly unfair at times, we all know that, but losing someone dear to you in such dire circumstances comes with its own baggage, I should imagine."

"He's going to be carrying around a lot of guilt when he returns. Any idea when that's likely to be?"

Sally entered the main entrance and glided into her parking space. "What are you saying? That you're fed up with me already and desperate to team up with Jordan again?"

"I hate it when you do that," Lorne replied once she was out of the car.

"Do what?"

"Surmise what is going on in my head. Invariably, you're wrong."

Sally pulled a face across the roof of the car. "Get you. Talking of Jordan… Will you guide him through his meeting at the prison for me? Make sure he has a list of questions to take with him. He needs to be fully prepared for the trip."

"I think your concern is unwarranted. I've been working with him a fair few months now, and he's a good copper. He thinks on his feet and shines like a beacon of knowledge when he has the wind behind him."

"A what? Beacon of knowledge?" Sally chuckled. "I've heard it all now."

"Stop taking the piss," Lorne hissed.

They entered the building with Sally still clutching at the stitch that had developed in her side. "You're incorrigible."

"If you say so."

They climbed the stairs, and once they entered the main office, Lorne headed over to the drinks station to fix them, and anyone else who wanted one, a drink.

"I'll be in my office. Give me half an hour to sift through the paperwork, and then we'll make a move."

"Do you want me to ring ahead, see if the next family are available to be interviewed?"

"Yes, do that. Maybe we should have made the arrangements last night before we left the station."

"I'm on it now. I can shift things around, see who is available and at what time."

Sally nodded. "It would be good to get them all out of the way today. Did you see the conference on the news last night?"

"I did. Want me to check if any calls came in?" Lorne asked.

"No, you contact the families. Joanna, can you chase up the desk sergeant, see if there have been any significant calls come our way yet?"

Joanna smiled and picked up the phone. Sally lingered by her doorway, waiting to hear the answer. But was disappointed.

"Nothing at all, boss."

"Jesus, don't people around these parts watch the news any more?" Sally didn't wait for a response. Instead, she closed the door and settled behind her desk. A wave of relief swept over her at the lack of contents in her in-tray to deal with.

Half an hour later, and she had mercifully finished the one daily chore that truly blighted her life. She returned to the outer office where she found Lorne and Jordan with their heads together.

"How's it going?"

Lorne sat back and said, "We're about done now. Jordan has jotted down all the necessary questions for his visit today."

"You'll nail it, Jordan. I have every faith in you." Sally smiled. "What time is your appointment?"

"Just after lunch, boss. I'm looking forward to it, or is that the wrong thing to say?" Jordan replied. He put down his pen and folded his arms.

"Depends if you've ever been to prison or not. Personally, I can't stand the places, they give me the chills, especially the one in Norwich, and we all know why. So I'm more than willing to hand over the reins in that respect. And how did you get on?" Sally asked Lorne.

Lorne opened her notebook and showed the itinerary she'd planned out for the day. "First one is in half an hour."

"Good, how far is it? In other words, do we have time to down a quick coffee before we hit the road? I don't tend to get up to speed in the morning until my caffeine levels are working at max, and I don't think they're quite there yet."

Lorne rose from her seat. "I can take a hint."

While Lorne fixed a fresh round of drinks, Sally brought the rest of the team up to date with the meetings they had held the day before with Gary and Jocelyn.

"What's your take on it, boss? Do you think the daughter is alive and living with her?" Jordan queried.

Sally shrugged. "Who knows? Let's see how things progress today with the other interviews and visit that later if we feel there's a need to."

* * *

"Is this the one, here?" Sally drew up outside a small row of terraced houses in yet another dodgy area, judging by the kids' toys strewn across the paths and the other trash littering the front gardens. "Nice to see people taking care of their community."

"Parents need to start them off young, that's what I did with Charlie. I bet she thought I was a right nag when I told her every day to 'put things back where they came from', but I reckon she's thanking me for it these days. Her place has always been immaculate."

"Good for her. Yes, I was brought up the same way. It's depressing to see neighbourhoods in such a state."

They left the car and weaved their way through the toys littering the front garden to the house they were visiting. Sally pulled the sleeve of her jacket over her finger and rang the bell. Nothing happened, so she knocked on the glass panel instead. A woman in her thirties, with dyed purple hair, opened the door and looked them both up and down.

"You must be the police. You'd better come in."

"Don't you want to check our ID first?" Sally asked.

"Not really. I was expecting you, so what would be the point? Anyway, it's not like I've got anything for you to take, is it? Look around you, most people living on this street don't have more than a fiver to their names. Harsh reality these days, ain't it?"

"Sorry to hear that. It's only going to get worse."

"Never mind, there's a good side to the cost-of-living crisis everyone is talking about." She stepped back and allowed them access to a surprisingly clear hallway.

"What's that?" Sally put a foot over the threshold, her nose already twitching at the unwelcome smell coming from the back of the house.

"It's going to keep the police on their toes. If you think the crime rate is high now, you just wait until the major energy price hike hits in October."

Sally shrugged. "I fear you could be right. We're aware of the situation."

"The question is, what are you doing about it?"

"There's not a lot we can do to prevent what's about to happen. Do you want us to take our shoes off?"

The woman laughed. "I wouldn't if I were you. This way, I'm just cooking up some tripe for later. It's all I can afford to feed the kids these days, and that's a special treat. I'm Gemma by the way."

"I'm DI Sally Parker, and this is my partner, DS Lorne Warner. Is it convenient for us to have a chat?"

"If you don't mind coming through to the kitchen. The smell might put you off, it's a bit of an acquired taste. No, change of plan, I can't put you through it. I'll switch it off and finish it later. We shouldn't be too long, should we?"

"I don't think so. Thanks, that would be great."

Gemma swiftly changed direction and squeezed past them. "This way it is then. I think it's reasonably tidy in here. If it's not, then you'll just need to accept it, sorry."

"Don't worry. We've seen a lot worse than this over the years."

The room was tidy enough, but the furniture had seen better days. The mismatched sofa and armchairs dominated the room, and there was a portable TV sitting on a trolley in the corner.

"Raising the kids alone has stretched me financially over the years. Mum and Dad do their best to chip in when they can, but the money they give is always for the kids' pocket money. I'd feel mean taking that off them, not that my parents can afford too much, living on a pension. Anyway, you don't want to listen to me going on. Why are you here? After five years of hearing zilch from you guys, I get a call to book an interview with me. Has something happened?"

"Did you watch the news last night or early this morning?" Sally teetered on the edge of the sofa next to Lorne while Gemma plonked herself in one of the faded green armchairs.

"No. I try and steer clear of it. Now and again Mum will ring me to tell me to switch the TV on if there's something of interest being aired, but that hasn't happened for a while. I tend to listen to my playlists most of the time. Why?"

"Fair enough. It's not obligatory. I held a press conference yesterday after a body was discovered in a lake."

"A body?" Gemma gulped. "Oh God, you're not telling me you think it's my sister, Lily, are you?"

"The remains are just that. It's going to be a while before the pathologist will be able to give us a formal identification. However, there were other items found with the remains which might help us in our investigation."

"What sort of things? Oh God, my heart is pumping hard here. What if this is Lily? In a lake, you said? I dread to think what condition the body is in, if it is her." She ran a hand over her cheek.

"I have a couple of photos."

Gemma's eyes widened in horror.

"Sorry, not of the remains but of the items found with the body. Will you take a look and tell me if you recognise them?"

"That's a bloody relief. My gag reflexes were on full alert for a minute there."

"I apologise." Sally left her seat and showed the different items to Gemma who remained nonplussed and shook her head.

"No, I don't recognise the material and haven't got a clue what that is."

"It's a belt buckle."

"No, sorry. You believe they belonged to the… what would you call them? Victim?"

"Yes. The remains were found in a hessian sack along with a few rocks and these items. We're presuming it was the victim's clothing that had survived being in the water for a length of time. Our pathologist is surmising the victim has been submerged in the lake for around five years."

"Ah, and that's why you've come to see me?"

"Yes. We checked our missing person' records and came up with five possible victims. We're working our way through the list now."

"Am I the first one you've visited?"

"No, you're the second. While we're here, would you mind going over what happened at the time of your sister's disappearance?"

"If I can. I've tried to block certain aspects out of my head over the years, I suppose for the kids' sake. The last thing they want to hear is me going on about their missing mother."

"I can understand that. Have you adopted the children?"

"Yes. I had to. Mum and Dad couldn't take them on, not at their age, neither of them is in good health. They help out now and again with babysitting duties, just to give me a break, but it's never enough. By the time I've got used to being alone they're back again. That's not to say I don't love them, but having them around has stifled me in more ways than I thought possible. I can't remember the last time I went out with a fella."

"You're amazing, not every family member would take on their sibling's children. I'm sorry you've had to put your life on hold, but you're to be admired, nonetheless. What happened with Lily?"

Gemma cast her eyes over to a picture of her with another young woman who looked very similar, the only difference being the colour of their hair. "I adored her. We used to be inseparable, there was no way I'd let her kids go into the system. Lily was on her way home from work. She'd not long started a part-time job after having the twins. Mum and Dad were fitter then, so they offered to take care of the kids for the three hours Lily worked in the evening. They used to go to her house and sit with the babies. When Lily failed to show up after her shift at the garage, Mum rang me. I went to the house. Mum was really upset, the twins were kicking off, crying for their mother. I retraced her steps back to the garage but found nothing. I rang the police, and they told me to ring back the next day or after twenty-four hours were up. That's a daft rule, you know in your gut when someone does something out of the ordinary."

"How old were the twins by then?"

"Six months."

"And was she suffering from post-natal depression?"

"Not as far as I know. She hadn't been to see the doctor, she would have told me. I went back to the garage. The girl there started her shift when it was time for Lily to leave. She told me she had arrived a couple of minutes late, but Lily was fine about it. I asked her if she had seen which way Lily went when she left. She told me she was serving a customer at the time Lily went home. I drove around the neighbourhood, walked the route several times and searched all the bushes, just in case someone had banged her over the head… and, you know… raped her. I found nothing. I reported it the next day, and the first thing the police did was arrest Eric."

Sally raised a finger. "Was that your sister's boyfriend or husband?"

"Yes, I should have mentioned him before. He was a useless toerag, lazing around while she went back to work. He got more living on the dole, that was his motto."

"And why didn't he take on the children, wasn't he the father?" Lorne asked. She offered Sally an apologetic smile for butting in.

"Yes, he was the father. He couldn't cope with the kids. As soon as I said I would help out, he buggered off."

"He left? Did the police track him down at the time, or did they let him go?"

"I need to rewind a bit, I'm jumping about all over the place. Like I said, I've tried to block it out over the years. The cops turned up and whisked him away for questioning. They thought he was behind her disappearance. But he was later released due to lack of evidence."

"I see. I'm guessing that didn't go down too well with Eric?"

"Not one bit. He ranted and raved about the injustice of it all, even blamed me at one stage for opening my mouth to the cops. I had to, something drastic had happened to my sister, and I wanted to get to the bottom of it. Five years later, and we're all still searching for clues."

"How did you feel about the police releasing Eric?" Sally asked, her mind whirling because of who the officer in charge of the case was at the time.

"I was confused about it. One minute I thought Eric had done something to Lily, but on the other hand, he seemed really cut up about what was going on. Not so cut up that he was prepared to stick around and help out with his kids, though, that's the part I can't forgive. What parent in their right mind would hand their kids over? Doesn't the love you have for them count for anything?"

"Indeed. Has he been in touch since? Seen the kids at all?"

"Nope. He went and has never returned. You're going to ask me where he is now, aren't you?"

Sally smiled and nodded. "Do you know?"

"No idea. Maybe you'll be able to find him."

"I take it he doesn't pay any maintenance towards the kids, then?"

"Ha, I'd bloody faint if he did. It sickens me how people don't have a problem producing kids, but when it comes to the crunch they don't want the responsibility of caring for them. It's down to people like me to put their lives on hold to save the day. Don't get me wrong, I don't regret taking the kids on but, bloody hell, everyone knows how much it costs to raise sprogs these days. I'm struggling, just like every other single mother is out there, and where are the fathers? Nowhere to be bloody seen. Sorry, I'm ranting now. I've bottled my emotions up for years, rather than let the kids know how I feel. They deserve so much better than I can give them. I fear for them most days. The constant worry of what will happen to them if anything bad comes my way. We haven't got a clue why Lily went missing or whether she is even alive today, but I have this fear that the same thing could happen to me, and then where would the kids be? I've already had a slight cancer scare."

"Have you? That's tough. Is everything all right now?"

"Yes, they picked up something in my latest smear test, but I had a small procedure and have been given the all-clear now. But who's to say what would have happened to the twins if things had been different?"

"Always a scary thought, dealing with cancer. It's so prevalent these days. They reckon it affects one in two of us… sorry, you probably know the stats more than me."

"Yes, I'm aware. I try not to think about it. Regular checkups for me from now on, that's a no-brainer in my opinion. Will you be able to trace Eric? I'd like to know if he's still around the area or not. Not that I want any contact with him, but you never know what the future holds for anyone."

"We can do some digging when we get back to the station. Eric what?"

"Eric Swallow. That's all I can give you."

"Don't worry. We'll do our best to try and find him in the system. Have you received any strange calls over the years?"

Gemma's temple furrowed. "Such as?"

"Someone calling you, pausing and then hanging up perhaps?"

"No, nothing that I can think of, and no one has contacted me asking for money either, if that's going to be your next question."

Sally smiled. "It was. I take it you weren't too impressed with how your sister's case was handled at the time."

"Not at all. The officer in charge appeared to dither a lot. I always felt he was way out of his depth. When I tackled him about it, he became defensive and warned me to back off if I wanted news about my sister in the future."

Sally shot Lorne a quizzical look and then turned her attention back to Gemma. "He said that? Warned you off?"

"Yep, it was done on the sly. Only me and him in the room. I felt intimidated by him. Did you ever meet him?"

"No, we've been going over his old cases for the past few years, and what we've uncovered… well, it's devastating, should never have been allowed to go on."

"A bent copper, is that what you're telling me?"

"His methods were questionable at times," she replied diplomatically.

"That's terrible. How the hell did he sleep at night? Did he fit innocent people up?"

"No comment, it's more than I dare do."

"Shocking to hear that goes on in the force. I can imagine it taking place years ago, when there were the likes of the Kray twins hanging around causing mischief. I saw a documentary about them years ago. I'm sure it said they had a few coppers in their back pocket at the time."

"They did. As a force, we've battled hard to correct the mistakes of the colleagues who have gone before us. At times, it has been a huge struggle."

"I'm not surprised. He was a vile man. Made me wary every time he chose to speak to me alone. Gave me the creeps, if I'm honest. I feel bad saying that out loud about a copper, but it's the truth."

"All I can do is offer my sincere apologies. I know it is too late and probably doesn't mean much."

"It's okay. I'm over it now. What grieves me is that he was in charge of my sister's case. I've often wondered if she might have been found, you know… if a woman had been in charge.

He gave me very little hope to cling on to but stopped short of telling me the likelihood of her being seen again was zero. My feelings didn't matter one iota in the end. I was livid when he let Eric go after questioning him for a few hours. I bet you would have detained him, wouldn't you?"

"Probably, but if there was no evidence at the time, there would have been no reason for us to have detained Eric. I know that's probably not what you want to hear."

"If it's the truth then fair enough, I just thought it was strange at the time. Where do we go from here?"

"We have other families we need to see, regarding the items found at the scene, but what I'll do for you is promise we'll go over your sister's notes after this investigation's over and carry out some extra digging for you. I can't promise we'll find anything, but it must be worth a try."

"And you're going to try and find Eric for me, as well?"

"Definitely. One way or another, if he's still in the country, he's bound to show up somewhere in the system. I'll let you know how we get on. We've got your number."

"And to think I was bricking it, you showing up today. I have to tell you, I deliberately chose to cook tripe just to turn your stomachs."

Sally and Lorne laughed.

"And who can blame you after your past experience?" Sally replied, her cheeks hurting after a few moments. "Falkirk was a one-off, I can assure you." She left her seat. "We'll let you get back to cooking now."

Gemma saw them to the front door. "Thank you for at least listening to me, which is more than the other fucker used to do. I feel a lot of time was wasted back then. Maybe if he'd got his act together quicker, Lily might have been found. All we can do is live in hope that she turns up one day, although, as time goes by, the likelihood of that happening is less and less, isn't it?"

"You must never give up hope. We'll be in touch soon. Thanks for agreeing to see us. Sorry if our meeting has caused you any distress."

"It hasn't, not really."

She closed the door gently behind them, and they walked back to the car.

"Another one bites the dust. I'm trying not to get worked up about what Falkirk did all over again, but it's so damn difficult. What a total arsehole. How dare he treat people as if they were beneath him and didn't have rights?"

"Hard to believe he got away with it for so long as well. All those cases… I hope his senior officer got into trouble when it all came to light."

Sally opened the car, and they got in. "I should have asked the question. The truth is, I was so incensed I forgot to, but yes, you're right, he shouldn't have been *allowed* to have got away with it in the first place. But that's a whole different proposition altogether, isn't it? Going after his senior officer… would we even want to go there? Have all that hassle to deal with?"

"Personally, no. I'd much prefer steering clear for a quiet life, however, it's the type of thing that is going to niggle my insides for a while."

"You must learn to switch off. Our records are exemplary. Unfortunately, other officers have been known to use their rank and status to their advantage. I could never live with myself or sleep at night if I did anything against the rules, not to that extent. Maybe I'm guilty of bending the rules in order to solve an investigation, perhaps that's how it all started with Falkirk in the first place. He found out how easy it was to mislead his senior officer and to manipulate the system."

"Everything snowballed, and he struggled to regain control perhaps? Not that I'm making excuses for the cockwomble. Christ, that's a word I haven't needed to use in a while."

Sally laughed. "I love it. Consider it my new name for the people of his ilk. Let's hope I don't have to use it that often in the future. In all seriousness, this situation does make you want to stand back and assess the system at times, doesn't it?"

"It really does. In all my years on the force in the Met, I think I only had to deal with police corruption once, and we can guess when that was... that criminal was a law unto himself and had the police, MPs, lawyers and even some judges under his wicked spell. Makes me shudder recalling what he did to my Charlie and the depths of evil he was capable of sinking to."

Sally reached for Lorne's arm. "Don't go there, love. Revisiting the worst period in your life never ends well. Take heart in what Charlie has become, a mini you. Fighting the worst criminals in society. She has to be one of the bravest people I know. I have a theory about the reason. Want to hear it?"

Lorne smiled at her with sparkling tears in her eyes. "Go on, surprise me."

Sally turned the key in the ignition and pulled away from the kerb. "Because she has the great Lorne Simpkins/Warner's genes running through her."

"Get away with you. She's twice the person I will ever be."

"Nonsense. She's inherited your grit, determination and willingness to right all the wrongs in this world. It takes a very special person to overcome what she was subjected to at the hands of that despicable tyrant."

"I know. Most young women would have crumbled, been unable to have gone on. To say I'm proud of her is a gross understatement. Shall we move on now?"

"Let's do it. Oh, and by the way, just for the record, I'm

proud to have you working alongside me. It's an honour I never thought I'd encounter again."

Lorne smiled. "Ditto. We're going to make a great partnership, if only a temporary one, until Jack returns to duty."

"Where are we off to next?"

Lorne entered the coordinates into the satnav, and Sally followed the automated voice's direction.

Once they were underway, Sally said, "Can you get in touch with Joanna, ask her to check for Eric Swallow in the system? I'd love to be able to get back to Gemma with a result, today. It'll go a long way towards repairing part of the damage caused by Falkirk."

Lorne placed the call and put the phone on speaker. Joanna promised to get on with the request and to search for an answer ASAP.

Not long after, they arrived outside a small cottage in one of the villages to the north of Wymondham, where they were based.

"And the husband is expecting us?" Sally asked.

"Yes, I was fortunate to catch him in when I made the appointment earlier. He told me he'd taken a few days off to be with his children."

"We'd better not hold him up too long then. We'll see if he recognises the belt buckle, and if he says no, we'll make our excuses just in case he decides to lecture us about how the case should have been dealt with under Falkirk."

However, once Tim Benjamin invited them into his lounge, Sally's good intentions went out of the window.

"It's about time someone got in touch with me after all these years. Don't tell me you've found her, have you?"

"First of all, I have to apologise for the lack of contact since your wife was reported missing, that should never have happened."

His eyes narrowed, and his welcoming smile had long

since disappeared. "But it did. You lot don't care about the people left behind, do you?"

"I can't apologise enough for the way you feel or for the way the officer in charge of the case treated you. The reason we're here is because we've discovered some human remains."

He gasped and took a step closer to her.

Sally held up a hand. "Please allow me to finish. I'm not for one second telling you that the remains belong to your wife. In all honesty, there's no way we'll be able to make an identification for a few days yet."

Tim shook his head. "I don't get it. Then why are you here? To get my hopes up only to dash them, or what?"

"We'd like to run a couple of items past you, see if you recognise them."

"Items? Such as? Why now, after all this time?"

"Because the items were found with the remains of the victim."

"And you're hoping I'll be able to recognise the damn things after all this time?"

Sally raised her crossed fingers. "Right now, it's all we have. Will you at least try?" She removed her phone from her jacket pocket and scrolled to the latest photos.

"Go on then, what have we got to lose?"

Sally showed him the images.

"What am I looking at here?"

"We believe it's a belt buckle. Did Tania ever wear belts?"

He shrugged. "How the heck do I know? It's been five years, and you expect me to remember what my wife used to wear?"

"What about the images of the cloth, anything? Something might jolt your mind. If not, then we'll have to leave it there."

He shook his head. "Nothing is coming to mind. What about her other shoe?"

Sally inclined her head and snuck a quick look at Lorne who seemed equally puzzled by his comment. "Sorry, her shoe?"

"Yes, it should have been in the file. One of her shoes was found by the river in Great Yarmouth a few days after I reported her missing."

"Ah, I must have overlooked that when I read the file."

Tim cocked an eyebrow and sighed. "Same old shit from the police. You're not there to help us, only to put obstacles in the way."

"I dispute that, it's grossly unfair. We're doing the best we can to solve a mystery, which is between four and six years old, with the evidence we have to hand."

His arms flew out to the sides and slapped against his thighs. "I'm sorry, you're going to have to forgive my lack of trust in the police, going by my past experience. I know the officer in charge suspected me when Tania went missing, even though she was on a night out with the girls over twenty miles away. He refused to listen to anything I told him, it was as if he was determined to see me go down for her murder, even though I had an alibi and Tania was out enjoying herself. He just wouldn't listen to me. Even threw me in a cell for a night, probably to rattle me, to unnerve me enough to sign a fake confession. That is how bent coppers work, isn't it?"

"We're sorry you were treated so appallingly. All I can say is things have changed over the years. Especially in this region."

"Because of what that shyster got up to?"

Sally sighed. "Yes, amongst other things. It wasn't our intention to come here today, to dredge up the awful memories you were forced to endure back then. All we're trying to do is identify a victim, who we thought might be your wife."

"Maybe it is and maybe it isn't. I'm sorry, but I can't help you. So where do we go from here?"

"Then we'll have to wait maybe days before the pathologist is able to give us a formal identification."

"And what if it's her, Tania? Will you come back here to arrest me?"

"For what?" Sally asked, confused.

"For not being able to identify the buckle or the items of clothing after all these years."

"No, not at all. I've accepted your reasons. Why don't we end this interview here? The last thing I wanted to do was cause you any unnecessary upset."

"Well, you have. Yes, I'm with someone else now, we can't get married, not yet, not until seven years have passed, but I have to tell you, when I close my eyes at night, Tania's face is the last thing I see. I often think about her, whether she died and was washed out to sea or whether someone kidnapped her and possibly people-trafficked her. I know that's extreme, but not when you consider what deplorable stories we hear in the news these days. I hope for her sake she has died and hasn't been subjected to a life of debauchery and sickening behaviour. I often sit and wonder what type of bloody world we're living in. I loved the very bones of that woman. I'm so pleased we decided to have children early, I cherish them and hold them tightly every single day, often shedding a tear that Tania isn't here today to see what beautiful souls they have. Life is unfair. We need to rid this world of all the vile people. They say there's a God up there. I used to believe it at one time, I used to go to church regularly when I was at school, but He failed me, like so many others. I'll probably get struck down for voicing my opinion now."

"You're not the first person to feel that way, Tim. All I can say is that until it has been proven otherwise, you need to cling on to the hope that Tania will come back to you one day."

He puffed out his cheeks and shook his head. "Crap, don't even go there. Can you imagine the disruption and heartache that would cause, what with me being with Vicky now?"

"Ah yes, I forgot about that small detail."

"I haven't." He laughed and showed them to the door. "I'm sorry for getting angry with you, I didn't mean to take it out on you."

"It's forgotten already. Take care."

Sally sighed heavily on the way back to the car. "This is all so depressing, having to spend most of our time apologising for someone else's failings."

"I know. Don't let it get you down, Sal."

"I'm trying not to. Who's next?"

# CHAPTER 4

The next house they tried they found no one home. Lorne tried to apologise, but Sally was having none of it.

"There might have been some kind of family emergency to tend to during the day, you know how accident-prone kids can be. Don't beat yourself up. We've still got one more family left to try, haven't we?"

"We have Zach Connor who is expecting us later, so it's touch and go if we'll find him in or not."

"We'll give it our best shot. Can you... it doesn't matter, here's Joanna now." Sally answered her mobile. "You're on speaker, Joanna, what have you got for us?"

"Hi. Right, I searched the electoral roll and DVLA for Eric Swallow and got a hit. I got in touch with his landlord, and he was a bit off with me, told me Swallow was in prison. So, I searched our records—sorry, I should have done that in the first place but had no reason to."

"It doesn't matter, Joanna. What did you find?"

"That he was put away for burglary. Several counts over a

few years were taken into consideration during the court case. He's serving a minimum of five years inside."

Sally's mind churned. "Okay, maybe the wheels fell off once his wife went missing, if he didn't have a record beforehand."

"He didn't, I checked," Joanna confirmed.

"Right, do me a favour. Jordan is at the prison now. Can you ask him if he'll slot in a visit with Swallow as well? I wouldn't mind hearing his side of things about the day Lily went missing. I believe he was arrested and later released due to lack of evidence against him. However, Gemma, Lily's sister, thinks the police gave up on him too soon. See what Jordan thinks, if Swallow is willing to speak with him."

"I'll get on to him now, boss. Want me to call you back or shall I just send you a text?"

"A text will do. We've still got two families we need to track down and interview before the end of the day. We're going to stop off and get some lunch as I've just seen the time. It tends to slip by when you're having fun… not."

Joanna laughed. "I bet. Stuart has nipped out to the baker's to get ours now. I wasn't about to look a gift horse in the mouth. First time he's offered to buy a sandwich in months."

"Good girl, grab the opportunity when you can, men can be so tight." Sally ended the call and pointed at the pub she had spotted down the road. "Fancy a pub lunch, on me?"

"Go on, I think you can twist my arm."

"Good. We deserve a break from all this doom and gloom. We needn't have much, not that I'm trying to wriggle out of paying, now that I've suggested it."

"Not sure if I could handle too much anyway, maybe a jacket potato or a sandwich. What do you think?"

"Sounds great to me."

Sally pulled into the car park, and they entered the characterful Ring of Bells via the main entrance.

The barmaid gave them a cheery smile and asked, "What can I get you?"

"Are you serving food still?" It was one forty-five by now.

"Yes, for another fifteen minutes. I'll get you a menu. Fancy anything to drink while you wait?"

"Orange juice for me," Lorne said.

"I'll have the same as we're still on duty."

The barmaid handed Sally a leather-bound padded menu. "On duty? Don't tell me you're with the police?"

"We are. We're not here on a professional matter, though, so no need for you to worry."

"Ah, well, it's good of you to pop in and see us." She flicked the top off two bottles of orange juice and placed a couple of ice cubes into two small glasses. "I should have asked if you wanted ice or not. Everyone's having it these days, what with the hot weather we're experiencing."

"It's fine, makes no odds to us. We'll take a seat and get back to you in a few minutes with our food order."

Lorne picked up the glasses, and Sally followed her to the table in the bay window, overlooking the river at the side of the property.

"Have you ever been here before?" Lorne asked.

"Once or twice. Do you like it here?"

"Yes, it's really quaint. We still haven't managed to get out much since we arrived."

"I'm not surprised, what with the renovations and running the kennel. Talking of which, have you found someone to run it yet?"

"We think so. She's starting on Monday. Nice girl, used to work at a kennel with her mother when she was younger. She's currently employed at a livery but is looking for a change. She's called Abby."

"She sounds ideal. What do you fancy?"

"I'll have jacket potato and tuna, please."

"I think I'll have cheese and beans."

"Have you ever tried pasta, beans and cheese? Out-of-this-world delicious."

"Really?" Sally asked, sceptical.

"Hey, don't knock it until you've tried it."

"I'll go and make the order before they decide to close the kitchen early. That'd be just our luck, wouldn't it?"

"PMA, boss."

Sally ordered at the bar and returned to her seat. Their lunch arrived around ten minutes later, and she and Lorne stared at the size of the meal placed in front of them.

"Blimey, I'm glad we decided to have something light and not a full meal," Sally said, her eyes bulging at the amount of cheese heaped on her plate.

"Enjoy, ladies. Maybe I should have warned you how large the meals are." The waitress giggled and left them to it.

"Damn, I hate wasting food but I'm going to have to, otherwise I'll be falling asleep during the interviews we have left this afternoon."

Lorne nodded. "I was thinking the same."

"Get stuck in, leave what you can't eat. You could always take the rest home to feed the dogs."

"Now there's a thought. Bon appetit!"

The conversation flowed while they huffed and puffed through their delicious lunch. They were both defeated about halfway through and shoved their plates away. The waitress came to collect their plates.

"Too much? I take it dessert is off the menu for you."

"Oh God, I don't want to see another ounce of food for the rest of the week, maybe the rest of the month," Lorne complained, clutching at her bulging tummy.

"You took the words out of my mouth. It was wonderful,

maybe I'll have the child's portion next time instead," Sally joked.

"Plenty of people say that. It makes sense if you don't have a healthy appetite," the waitress agreed.

"That's the trouble, I usually don't have a problem throwing excessive portions down my neck, but that beat me ten times over."

The waitress left the table, and they finished off their drinks.

"Are you fit?" Sally asked.

"Fit to leave or fit to drop? I think the latter might be on the cards this afternoon after that feast."

The barmaid waved as they walked to the door. "See you again soon."

"You will. Compliments to the chef," Sally replied. She pushed open the door and took in a large gulp of fresh air once they were standing on the steps outside. "That's us replete and ready for action once more."

Their next stop was Nicola Connor's father. They found him waiting for them at the downstairs window of a new detached home on a select estate nearing completion.

"Nice area. I think all new-builds should be like this, small and well spaced. Unfortunately, it never turns out that way. I couldn't stand living on a new estate where all the houses are on top of each other. It was bad enough when I left Daryl and had to move back in with my parents for a little while. I still cringe at the nightmare neighbours we had to contend with back then. Still, that's a different story. What I'm trying to say is give me a place like yours and mine any day and I'd be as happy as a pig in muck, or maybe this place. It seems quite nice, or it will be once the developer has moved off site."

"Definitely one of the nicer new-builds I've seen lately. Maybe they're for executive families, so that came with a premium price."

"I fear you're right. Let's get in there and see what the father has to say."

Sally didn't get the chance to ring the bell because Mr Connor was already standing on the doorstep, wearing jeans and a crisp white T-shirt along with an anxious smile.

"Hello, Mr Connor. I'm DI Sally Parker, and this is my partner, DS Lorne Warner. Thank you for agreeing to see us today."

"It's good of you to contact me. I haven't heard from the police in years. I have to tell you that I have mixed feelings about your visit. Please, come in. Sorry, I hope you don't find this a cheeky request, but if you wouldn't mind removing your shoes."

"Not at all, I was about to ask you that very question," Sally replied.

They removed their shoes and left them on the doormat, then he showed them into a spacious, pristine lounge. Three of the walls were painted white, and the final one was decorated in what appeared to be a Mackintosh design wallpaper, going back to the Arts and Crafts movement. The effect was stunning, even to Sally's untrained eye. She glanced sideways and caught Lorne casting an interested eye over the pattern.

"This is beautiful. Have you been here long?" Sally enquired.

"Thank you. It was my wife's idea. She said if we didn't add a bit of colour the white walls would close in on her and make it seem like we were on a hospital ward. I couldn't see it myself, but she's happy with the result. She'll be thrilled you like it."

"Is your wife around, sir?"

"It's Zach. No, she went to Norwich, shopping for

curtains this morning. Experience is telling me not to expect her back anytime soon. Please, won't you take a seat? Can I get you a drink?"

"We're fine, thanks all the same. My partner called you this morning to make this appointment and told you that we would need to discuss your daughter's case."

"That's right. Has there been a development, is that what you're saying?"

"Possibly. I'm going to have to ask you to try to remain calm, if you will."

"Of course. Now my stomach is churning. Please, don't keep me dangling any longer."

Sally inhaled a large breath and let it seep between her lips slowly. "Well, I'm not sure if you saw the news bulletin I put out recently, or not?"

He frowned, appearing thoughtful.

"A few days ago we discovered some remains."

He sighed and ran a hand over his face. "Oh my. Is it her? Is it Nicola?"

"Regrettably, we won't be able to divulge the victim's identity for a while. However, we had a number of items that were found in the sack that might help us with the identification process."

"What were they? Wait, where was the body found?"

"In Cavendish Lake. It's dried up at the moment. The sack was found in what would have been the centre of the lake, weighted down with stones. I have some photos… of the items we need to identify, if you're willing to take a look?"

"I'd be a fool not to. I need to know what happened to my daughter, to find closure after all these years."

Sally left her seat and showed him the photo of the belt buckle on her phone. "Do you recognise this?"

"Is it a buckle?"

Sally confirmed with a nod.

"No, I don't recall her ever wearing a belt," he said.

Sally flicked through the photos to the fabric samples they'd found at the scene. "This is probably going to be a long shot... What about these?"

He stared at the images for a while and then said, "No, I'm sorry, yet another blank."

Sally returned to her seat beside Lorne and said, "It's okay. We have five families in the area, all with relatives reported missing around the time the pathologist believes the body was placed in the water. It's all we have to go on right now."

"Will we ever know what happened to Nicola? I've lived with the torment of knowing that she might still be alive and unable to get back to us for the past five years. I assure you, it doesn't get any easier with every passing year."

"I'm sure it can't be easy. I've asked the other families this question, have you ever had any calls where someone has failed to answer?"

"No. Nothing along those lines, if I had, I would have known it was Nicky trying to reach out. We were a very close family. I still go out there searching for her. It took me years to pluck up the courage to move house and get on with my life, but I will never forget her. My old neighbours have our new address, they've told me they will keep an eye open for anyone visiting the old house, just in case she shows up. I have a feeling that she's alive, out there somewhere, in need of my help."

"I can only imagine the torment and suffering a family in your position goes through. I have to ask, were you treated well at the time your daughter went missing?"

"I don't understand. In what respect?"

"By the police investigating Nicola's disappearance."

"Is that in any doubt?"

"Maybe. The other families we have spoken to felt they weren't treated right during the investigation."

He paused to consider Sally's statement and shrugged. "I can't say that it ever crossed my mind. Maybe the lack of updates over the years was something I hadn't counted on. I have called the station regularly in the past five years, only to be told that there has been no further news in my daughter's case."

"I see. Is there anything else you need to ask us?"

"I don't think so. This body you've found, I take it it's female?"

"We believe so. As you can imagine, it is in poor condition and will need to be examined extensively by the pathologist and her team. I have every confidence she will be able to identify this person soon. All we're trying to do is jump ahead a little, rather than sit around doing nothing."

"That's great to hear. I'm sure the family concerned will be grateful for your commitment after all these years."

"It's part of our job, sir. I should have introduced myself properly. I'm in charge of a Cold Case Team that was set up in the area a few years back."

"Ah, it's all making sense now. If this person isn't my daughter, does this mean that you and your team will be investigating all the old cases that have remained unsolved?"

Sally winced. "Sadly, the force doesn't have the resources to go over every unsolved case, not unless we stumble across an incident such as this. I know that's not what you want to hear at this stage."

"I appreciate your honesty and understand what it's like working under such restrictions. It doesn't help the families going through the torment of not knowing what happened to their loved ones or whether they're likely to return one day."

"I get that. All I can do is give you my word that if we get the chance to go over your daughter's case in the near future, we will."

"Thank you, that means a lot. I sit here racking my brains most days, trying to remember if Nicky had anything troubling her at the time she went missing, but I keep drawing a blank. We were very close, I'm sure she would have told me if she had any issues going on in her life."

"Was Nicky an only child?"

"No, she has a younger sister, Fiona. She was devastated at the time. I'm not sure if she's ever recovered to be honest with you. Unfortunately, she has tried on more than one occasion to end her life. She's on antidepressants, and they've changed her dramatically. She was such a carefree child, and now, she spends every waking moment looking over her shoulder in case someone abducts her. I dread to contemplate what might be going on in that head of hers, but I know she wouldn't be going through all of this if nothing had happened to her sister."

"That's so sad, and my heart truly goes out to you. I take it she's had counselling?"

"Yes, she's under the specialist. She's been sectioned a few times. To tell you the truth, I've been at the end of my tether with her for years. On the one hand, I'm doing all I can to find one missing daughter while I'm gradually losing another daughter to this strange and debilitating illness."

"Life is so unfair. I would hate to be in your shoes, living with the unknown."

"Yes, on top of living with our normal daily lives that can be fraught at times as certain things arise. Only last month my wife had a nasty prang in the car when a youth stole a car and was being chased by the police. It's just one thing after another, or so it seems. I'm sure everyone goes through life saying that at one time or another, don't they?"

"I'm sure you're not alone in thinking that. Maybe some people are tested more than most in this life."

"I can vouch for that. Anyway, enough of me feeling sorry for myself, I must let you get on. I hope you find the lucky family, no, that came out wrong, the family who can finally lay their loved one to rest."

"We hope so, too. We have one final throw of the dice before we have to go back to the drawing board and start all over again."

"I don't envy you, it must be a real toll for you to encounter every day. Thank you for taking the time to come and see me, and for even thinking about our Nicky."

"You're welcome. I'm sorry the news wasn't better, but it also gives you something to cling on to as well, I hope."

He placed a hand over his heart. "I know she's out there somewhere, I feel it here every day."

Sally and Lorne slipped their shoes back on and said farewell.

"That was another heartbreaking tale," Lorne said on the way back to the car.

"I wish we could help them all find their loved ones. The truth is, as past experience tells me, some people choose to go missing with the intention of never being found again."

"That's a real shame. I'd love to know what goes on in people's heads when they are forced to make such a life-changing decision."

"It depends on what they've had to deal with. There are certain circumstances where I think it is warranted."

"Abuse cases, is that what you mean?"

"Yes, I bet there are thousands of women out there who have had to reinvent themselves as it were, in order to remain safe and alive."

Lorne raised a finger. "Maybe, but don't they tend to take their children with them? Regarding all the families we've seen over the past few days, none of the women took their little ones."

"Granted. That's why these types of cases are sometimes impossible to get our heads around."

"Makes sense. It's all so frustrating. We've got one final shot. Let's hope Steve Morton can identify the items and we get the break we need."

"PMA."

## CHAPTER 5

After leaving Mr Connor's stunning new-build, Morton's house was a stark contrast. It was a semi-detached, brick-built, half-rendered property on a very large estate near Dereham.

"Let's hope he's home," Lorne said.

They entered the front garden which was overgrown and had a few flowering shrubs being strangled by that sticky weed with the unpronounceable name that tended to spread like wildfire if it wasn't dealt with immediately.

Sally rang the bell which failed to work, so she tapped the knocker a few times instead.

A man in his mid-thirties, sporting fashionable bumfluff on his chin, greeted them with a wary expression. "Yes. Who are you?"

"Hello, Mr Morton. I'm DI Sally Parker, and this is my partner, DS Lorne Warner. Would it be possible for us to come in and speak with you? We tried contacting you earlier but didn't receive a response."

"About?"

"It's a delicate matter, sir."

He turned his back and walked up the hallway, expecting them to follow. Sally hesitated at the door, took a moment to consider removing her shoes, then decided against it when she glanced around the area and didn't see any others lying around.

"I wouldn't bother," Lorne whispered as if reading her mind.

Sally smiled and went in search of Mr Morton who was in the kitchen, preparing an evening meal for his children. Two little boys were at the table in fits of giggles, bashing their cutlery on the round pine table.

"What have I told you about doing that, Haydon and Rory? It'll be ready when it's ready and not before." He glanced at Sally and Lorne. "Can you give me five minutes just to dish up, and then we can sit down and talk?"

"That's fine. Take your time. Is there anything we can do to help while we're here?"

"Actually, there is. I forgot to pour the kids a drink, would you mind?"

"In the fridge?" Sally asked.

"Yes, orange juice. The glasses are in the cupboard on the right."

Sally removed two small glasses and opened the fridge to collect the carton of juice. "Here you go, children, enjoy. Not too much, it'll fill you up and you won't eat your dinner." She placed the glasses, one in front of each child, and stood back.

"Thanks, I'm always telling them that but they rarely listen." He dished up their dinners, which consisted of chicken nuggets, beans and chips cooked in the air fryer, and delivered them to the table. "We'd be lost without the air fryer, wouldn't we, boys?"

"Love our chips, Daddy," the older boy said.

"We do, Haydon. Can I get you a drink, ladies?"

"No, we're fine, thanks all the same."

"Shall we go through to the lounge?" Morton asked.

Lorne hesitated. "Do you want me to stay here and watch over the children? They seem a little young to be allowed to fend for themselves."

Sally cringed.

Morton looked Lorne up and down and shouted, "Are you trying to tell me how to bring up my kids?"

"No, sorry. I wouldn't dream of it. Forget I mentioned it."

Morton stormed out of the kitchen, and Sally and Lorne followed. Lorne mumbled an apology which Sally waved away.

"Don't be daft, you were only looking out for the kids. It's down to him if anything happens to them or the place is a mess after they're left to their own devices for a while."

"We're bound to get the blame either way."

The lounge was neatly presented, a few kids' toys strewn in the corner, but in the main, the room was exceptionally clean and tidy, considering there was a man and two boys living there.

"Take a seat. The sooner we get this over with the sooner you can leave. How dare you enter my house and get on your high horse with me?" His statement was aimed at Lorne.

"I'm sorry. I only said it out of concern for the children, I didn't mean to cause offence."

"Well, you did. Do you have children? Grandchildren?"

Mortified, Lorne nodded. "A grown-up child. That doesn't prevent me from remembering what a handful she was at mealtimes. Again, I'm sorry for my lack of judgement."

"Accepted. The boys are pretty good. They're best of friends, I never have any serious bother with them."

The three of them sat.

Sally cleared her throat and asked, "Do you have anyone special in your life these days, Mr Morton?"

"No. There aren't many women out there who are willing

to take on another woman's children, no matter how good they are."

"Sorry to hear that," Sally replied. "Are you up to answering a few questions about your wife's disappearance?"

"Why? After all these years? Wait a minute, haven't I seen you on the news lately?"

"That's right. We're here in connection with the press conference I put out the other day. I take it you didn't recognise any of the items I showed the cameras?"

"I didn't see anything. I think I was dealing with the kids at the time and only caught a glimpse of you on the screen for a second or two before one of the boys needed me for something or other. What did you show?"

Sally left her seat and showed him the photo of the belt buckle and the images of the cloth that were found at the scene.

He stared at the images and flipped back and forth between them a couple of times. Then he nodded.

"What's wrong? Do you recognise them?" she asked, her heart skipping several beats.

"They look familiar, I think. I'm not one hundred percent sure, though." The colour in his cheeks paled.

"Are you all right, Mr Morton?"

"It's Steve. I'm not sure, I think I'm going to be sick." He rushed out of the room and left Sally and Lorne staring at each other.

"We could be on to something here," Lorne whispered.

"Let's not get too excited just yet."

Lorne took the opportunity to return to the kitchen to check on the boys who were silently tucking into their meals. "Enjoying it?"

"It's yummy going down into my tummy," the little one said.

Lorne smiled. "We'll be next door if you need us, okay?"

The boys nodded, and Lorne joined Sally.

"See, they're fine, aren't they?" Sally asked.

"Amazingly, yes. They appear to be on their best behaviour."

With that, Steve returned to the lounge. "Sorry about that. Glad I hadn't eaten, I would have brought it all up. As it was, I just brought up a bit of bile. Too much information, I know. Forgive me."

Sally smiled. "There's really nothing for us to forgive. It must have come as a huge shock to you after all this time."

"I'm still not sure they're my wife's but I know she had a buckle like that. I had to take it to the cobbler's in town, he put it on a belt for us. She used to wear it all the time. The one concern I have is whether she wore it to the gym or not the night she went missing."

"Ah, that's understandable. Studying it, we believe it to be a unique piece."

"That's why Gail liked it so much. I think her brother bought it for her as a gift. She adored things that were distinctive. Special items to add to her collection."

"This is a long shot, but do you still have all of her clothes here?"

"Yes, I could never throw them out."

"Some family members might consider donating clothes and belongings to a charity rather than have them sit there as a constant reminder."

"No, it was suggested at the time, by her mother, but I refused to do it. Maybe I wanted to cling on to the hope of seeing her again."

"Okay. In that case, would you be willing to search through your wife's drawers and wardrobe to see if you can find the belt?"

"That's a great idea. Do you want to help me? It might lessen the blow emotionally to have someone there with me.

I moved out of the main bedroom the week she went missing and have barely set a foot back in there since."

"If that's what you want. It'll get the job done quicker. Lead the way," Sally replied, her heart pounding faster as the anticipation grew.

Steve hesitated at the door to the bedroom and sucked in a steadying breath before he entered the room.

Sally reached out and touched his arm. "Take your time, there's no rush."

"Oh God, the kids. They shouldn't be left alone, not for this long."

"I'll go," Lorne volunteered. "If that's all right with you?"

"Thank you. You're too kind, considering the way I spoke to you downstairs."

Lorne smiled. "It's all in a day's work."

"We shouldn't be too long," Sally said.

Lorne set off. Steve and Sally watched her disappear out of view, and then Steve plucked up the courage to enter the room with Sally right behind him.

"You've got this," she said.

"I hope so. She meant the world to me. I've done my very best with the children, to honour her name."

Sally smiled. "From what I can tell, they're an absolute credit to you. You've done an excellent job of raising them, teaching them good manners and how to behave properly at such a young age."

"Thank you," he muttered. He opened one of the drawers and stared at the contents for a while. "This was her accessories drawer, you know, for belts et cetera."

Sally observed the pattern of his breathing change, and there was an urgency to search the drawer. "Hey, there's no rush. Take your time, you're going to need to be thorough."

"I know what I'm looking for." He got to the bottom of the drawer, glanced her way and shook his head.

"Okay, we can't give up at the first hurdle. Maybe the belt was still attached to a pair of jeans or some trousers. Do you want me to search her wardrobe?"

There was a moment's pause from him, and then he gave her the go-ahead. "Okay, I'll look in the other drawers, see if she put it in one of those by mistake." He squatted to carry out the search.

Sally nodded and opened the sliding door of the fitted wardrobe that took up one of the alcoves. She snuck a peek at him every now and again and caught him sucking in extra breaths, she assumed to calm his erratic heart rate. She totally understood the roller-coaster of emotions the poor man must have been going through.

*This exercise must feel like torture to him.* "How are you holding up, Steve?"

He stood and ran his hands down the legs of his jeans a few times. "Sweaty palms, racing heart. I suppose it's to be expected, right?"

"There's no need to rush. I totally understand what you must be going through. We'll do this in your own time." Sally returned to flick through the hangers and stopped at yet another pair of trousers to check the waistband. Nothing there. Out of the corner of her eye she saw Steve take a deep breath and crouch in front of the chest of drawers again.

"I'm going in," he said, proud of his exploits.

Sally didn't say anything in response. They hadn't been at it long when tiny feet could be heard clambering up the stairs. Steve rushed towards the door to prevent his sons entering the room.

"Did you eat all your dinner, boys?" Steve raised his head to look at Lorne behind them, and she nodded.

"Every last mouthful. They're bugging me for ice cream. I told them they'd better ask you first, hence them coming up to see you. I tried to stop them, but excitement got the better of them."

"It's fine. They do love their ice cream. Give me five minutes to do what I have to do for this nice lady," he threw a thumb over his shoulder in Sally's direction, "and I'll be right down."

"Ohhhh... Dad. Can't we have it now? I can do it," Haydon said.

Steve smirked and ruffled his son's hair. "I know, but that tub has to last us all week, or at least until I can find the time to go shopping again. I doubt if that will happen if you go around helping yourself, matey. Now scram, and be patient, unless..." His gaze rose to latch on to Lorne's.

She smiled. "Say no more. Leave it to me. Come on, boys, now we've been given the green light, let's go find you some ice cream." Lorne held out her hands, and the boys slipped their tiny ones into hers and then yanked her back down the stairs.

"Hey, go steady," Steve warned. He returned to his chore and shook his head. "They can be so boisterous at times."

"They're adorable. Have they found it hard over the years?"

"I've done my very best to be there for them when they've needed me."

"What about any extra help? I hope you weren't stubborn enough to turn it down."

"No, definitely not. I know my limitations. Jan, that's Gail's mum, has been an absolute diamond. She's been there every step of the way, for all of us."

"What about your own family?"

"I don't have any. That's why I've become so reliant on Jan and Andrew, Gail's father, over the years."

"It's good that they've chipped in and helped out. It saved you struggling on your own. Do you work?"

"Yes, from home, thanks to the lockdown. It gave me the freedom to start working from home, which was a success. Even though I had Haydon and Rory under my feet most of the time, my boss said if anything, my work rate had improved and he was more than happy for the arrangement to continue."

"That must ease the pressure on your shoulders. I'd love to work from home, but I can't see that happening anytime soon." Sally sniggered. "You're lucky to have Gail's family around you to help out."

"I know I am. Jan is a real sweetheart. Sometimes she'll turn up laden down with homemade goodies, like lasagne, cottage pie, which the kids adore, or even dozens of cupcakes to see them through the week. I've never been good in the kitchen. I'm getting better, but she knows how and when to supply the support, when I need it most."

"They're her grandchildren, it's what grandparents do. I'm so glad you're still in touch with them. No doubt their support has been a great source of comfort to you and the kids over the years."

"It has, definitely. We always spend birthdays and Christmas together. The boys get so excited when packing up their bag to go off to Nanny and Granddad's house."

"Something to look forward to. We'd better crack on. How are you feeling now?"

"Less anxious. Thanks for the chat. Women are so intuitive to other's needs."

Sally blushed. "Sometimes, not all the time, but I do my best. I haven't found the belt yet, but I have found several tops similar in colour to the fabric sample we found at the scene."

"Sounds about right. If I remember rightly, Gail used to go through stages of buying several tops in similar tones so that she could mix and match more outfits. It must be a gender thing, I just grab the nearest T-shirt and shove it on. Don't even bother to think if it goes with the jeans I'm wearing or not."

"Hey, don't put yourself down, I do the same when I'm wearing jeans. There are no set rules with denim. Not that I'm an aficionado where fashion is concerned."

"I hear you."

They got back to work. The chore lasted another ten minutes but, in the end, they both drew a blank.

"Hey, don't look downhearted," Sally said and then chewed on her lip, realising what she had just said and the consequences to the alternative.

"Why shouldn't I? I'm intelligent enough to know what our failure means, Inspector."

"Yes, I know. I apologise, I didn't realise what I was saying until it was too late."

"It's okay. I think. What does this mean now? That you've made a positive identification? That my wife is officially dead… gone, never to be seen again?"

"Let's not get carried away. It's true, we believe the belt buckle was a one-off, but let's not be too hasty in believing the corpse we discovered is that of Gail. There are still tests to be carried out. All it means is that we might possibly be one step closer to finding out the truth."

He fell silent and stared at the floor in front of him, letting her words sink in. His head slowly rose, and his gaze met hers. Unshed tears glistened under the overhead light. "This means I'm going to have to break Jan's heart. That woman has held on to the hope of seeing Gail for so many years now, this news could destroy her."

Sally shook her head and raised a hand. "Let's get one thing straight here, you don't have to be the one to break the news. I can do it. I'd be more than willing to, if it will save both of you extra grief."

"Thank you, that would mean a lot to me. I'm not sure I could cope with the rejection she might dish out. Who knows how she is likely to react?"

"It's not going to be easy. There's nothing simple about this scenario. Maybe it would be best to avoid say anything until the formal identification has taken place and the pathologist gives us the all-clear."

He chewed his lower lip and shook his head. "I don't think that would be right, keeping the news from her. If she finds out that I knew and said nothing, I think it would ruin our relationship. For the sake of the boys, I don't think I'm willing to go down that route."

"You know best."

He peered over his shoulder at the bed and then took two steps back and lowered himself onto the edge of it. "I feel totally drained, my insides are numb. Is that normal? How should I feel?"

"No one knows in such circumstances because everyone registers different emotions. I suppose it's even harder to determine how people should feel or react when their loved one vanished five years before."

"You're not kidding. We've held on to the hope of her walking back through the door, and now... that's gone."

"Let's not jump ahead just yet. I'm going to need to ring the pathologist, give her the heads-up about what's going on."

"Do you want to use the phone? No, of course you don't, you'll have your mobile with you. See, the brain fogginess has already begun."

Sally took a step towards him. "Don't be so hard on yourself. You're going to have to allow yourself to grieve. Don't add an extra burden to your shoulders. My advice would be to deal with the different emotions as they materialise. Don't let things escalate out of control."

"I'll do that." His hands covered his face and slid down his neck. "How the hell am I going to tell the kids? What if they hate me after I tell them?"

"See, you mustn't think like that. They hold too much love for you to ever hate you, Steve. You've done a fantastic job over the years, holding this family together." Sally's heart squeezed with the anguish ahead of the man sitting in front of her, who had done his utmost to keep things 'normal' for his kids' sake.

He inhaled and exhaled deep, shuddering breaths. "I feel like one of those heavy weights they used to demolish buildings has just rammed into my chest. Will I ever recover from her loss?"

Sally touched his shoulder. "In time. I know how hard this must be for you right now, no words I can say could possibly ease that pain. You're going to need to have time alone, to go through the grieving process all over again. But to add a word of caution, we're going to need to get a proper identification first."

He placed a clenched fist to his chest. "I feel it here. I know she wouldn't have upped and left the boys. I've always felt that something bad had happened to her. Will we ever find out how she died? You said on TV that the remains of a body had been discovered in a sack in a dried-up lake, didn't you?"

"That's correct."

His brow wrinkled. "My mind is thinking all sorts of dark thoughts, like how does a body get put in a sack in the first place, was it a large one, the size of a Santa sack that I fill each year for the kids?"

"No, it was one half the size. The lab is running tests on it as we speak. I'm hopeful they'll have a result for us soon. However, if the sack and its contents have been in the water for around five years, you can imagine what kind of impact that is going to have on the result."

"I get that, I think. I've got an image of Gail being shoved into the sack in a foetal position, but I'm being delusional, aren't I?"

Sally paced the floor, debating whether to tell him the truth or not, fearing what would happen if she did. "The truth is, it's hard to know how she was put into the sack or the water. Why don't we take a moment and step back from letting our thoughts get the better of us? Playing out all the possible grisly scenarios isn't going to help either you or the children to cope with the situation."

"Maybe you're right. What happens next, with regard to the family? You're not going to force us to see her, are you?"

"No, we would never entertain doing that. Usually, in cases like this, a post-mortem is performed to establish the cause of death and then the remains will be sent straight to the funeral home."

"Heck, that's something I hadn't even thought about, the funeral. Where do you even begin, after all this time…?"

"There's no rush. It's something you can take your time to consider, as a family. The examination and all the tests that need to be carried out could take weeks to complete."

"Maybe Jan and Andrew will help me."

"I'm sure they will. I bet you won't even need to broach the subject with them. They sound like genuinely decent people who only want what's best for you and their grandchildren."

He let out a long, exasperated sigh. "They do. My mind is racing, and I need to find a way of stopping it hurtling out of control."

"Take a few deep breaths, to calm yourself. We can hang around, we've got no intention of leaving you high and dry after delivering this kind of news."

"Thank you. Can we leave this room now? I don't think it's doing my soul the power of good being in here, knowing that she's gone for good."

"I was about to suggest the same. I don't know about you, but suddenly, I'm in dire need of a cuppa."

"Or a shot of something alcoholic in my case."

"Feel free, I'd join you if I wasn't on duty."

They walked out of the room, Steve locked the door on his way out and put the key on the doorframe above. "I want to thank you for your kind words."

"It's all part of the job."

He tilted his head. "Is it? I'm getting the impression that you are one of a kind, Inspector."

"Not at all." Sally took the lead down the stairs and sneakily wiped a tear from her eye at the bottom.

They entered the kitchen to find Haydon and Rory scraping the remains of the ice cream from the bowls.

"I only gave them one scoop," Lorne said.

"Did you enjoy it, boys?" Steve asked, ruffling their hair again.

"It tasted nicer when the lady gave it to us, Daddy," Haydon said.

They all laughed.

Steve touched a clenched fist to his son's arm. "How to put a dent in your father's confidence. Thanks for that, son."

"Sowwy, Daddy. I like this lady, can you marry her?"

Lorne and Sally looked at each other and burst out laughing.

"I think my husband will have something to say about that, Haydon," Lorne replied.

"Crikey, if ever I wanted the ground to swallow me up, it's now. You need to watch what you're saying, Haydon, and stop trying to embarrass your poor old dad."

Lorne waved her hand. "No harm done, don't worry."

"I'll put the kettle on and have a blush in the corner, where you can't see me."

"Two coffees, white, one sugar, please," Sally said, suppressing a smile. "I'm just going to make a call in the hallway, Steve. Lorne, can you come with me?"

They left the room and closed the door behind them.

"Are we sticking around?" Lorne whispered.

"I told him we had no intention of rushing off. He was in a bit of a state upstairs, struggling to control the wayward thoughts entering his mind."

"Are you saying that you believe his wife is the victim?"

"Yes, sorry. We couldn't find the belt upstairs, and I noticed a few clothes which appeared to have a similar design to the fabric we found. I'm going to ring the pathologist now to let her know."

"I'll give you some space to do that then. Shall I go back in there and sit with Steve and the kids?"

"You appeared to have hit it off with the children."

"Hard not to, they're adorable, and no, that's not me getting broody."

"Did I say anything?" Sally smirked and removed her phone from her pocket. "I shouldn't be too long. We'll see how he's faring while we have a drink and then shoot off."

"Okay."

Sally rang Pauline's mobile number.

The pathologist answered on the second ring. "Hello, is that you, Sally?"

"It is, Pauline. I have news for you." Sally moved away from the kitchen towards the front door. "We believe we've traced the victim's family."

"Cool. How?"

"We trawled through the missing person list for anyone who was reported missing around five years ago. We came up with five possible names and, would you believe it, the last relative we tried has come up trumps. The husband thought he recognised the belt buckle, and we've spent the last half an hour searching through the woman's wardrobe. Nothing there. But I did find several items of clothing that could match the pieces of cloth also found in the bag."

"If you're happy to proceed, then we can obtain the dental and medical records for the victim and make the comparisons. Want me to put a halt on the anthropologist now?"

"My gut is telling me yes."

"I agree. Can you pave the way for us and get the all-clear from the victim's family to obtain the necessary records? I've already got the bone DNA process underway."

"I'll broach the subject with the husband right away."

"Thanks. Do we need to discuss anything else?"

"I can't think of anything. Oh, I suppose I should ask how the PM and tests are coming along."

"One-word answer to that question... slowly. I've had a couple of other scenes in the county I've needed to attend to, so I was forced to put your PM, so to speak, on hold. However, the initial tests were carried out more or less as soon as we brought the remains back to the lab."

"I'll leave it with you and send you a text with the doctor's and dentist's details later."

"I'd appreciate it, and then we can get on with what's needed to corroborate the ID. Good speaking to you again, Sally. If I don't talk to you before, have a good weekend. And don't ask, I probably won't get one because of all the cases that need dealing with, all marked as urgent, as usual."

"That's a shame. Maybe you should start as you mean to go on and put your foot down from the outset."

"Can I send all the irate officers, whom I'm likely to piss off by doing that, in your direction?"

"Ugh... I'd rather you didn't. I can't handle irate officers these days. All the team members I've pulled together are pretty laid-back, except for Jack, my partner, but I've got the measure of him and keep him on a tight leash."

"I thought as much when I met him the other day."

"I mustn't speak ill of him, he's on bereavement. His father has just died in an accident."

"Oh, my goodness. How dreadful. Locally?"

"No, down south."

"Send him my best regards if you speak to him. Do you have an adequate stand-in available?"

"I will, and yes. Lorne Warner has stepped up to the plate. She's quite new to the team but she has dozens of years' experience under her belt. She used to be a DI with the Met."

"Lorne? That's unusual. Hmm… it seems to ring a bell. I did a stint down there whilst I was training. Let me think… Hang on a second, something's coming back to me. I've got it. Did she have any dealings with Jacques Arnaud, the pathologist down in London?"

"Oh gosh, that's going back a few years. Yes, you have a good memory."

"He had a huge impact on my career at the time. A wonderful man, full of himself, but a terrific pathologist nonetheless. It was a travesty when he lost his life, totally unexpected."

Sally relived the events surrounding Jacques' death and the personal devastation it had caused to Lorne at the time. "I remember it all too well. Still, we really mustn't dwell on the past. Hopefully the future will be much brighter for all of us while we get to know one another."

"Let's hope so. It just shows you how alert we all have to be in our line of work."

"Indeed. I'll be in touch soon." Sally returned to the kitchen to find the boys had left the table. Steve was at the sink washing the dishes, and Lorne was over on the sofa, reading to the children who were sitting either side of her, captivated by the way she was reading *The Wonky Donkey* to them. Sally crossed the room to the sink and picked up a tea towel.

"You don't have to do that," Steve said, shocked.

"I know. But if we can lend a hand while we're here, it's fine by us. How are you feeling?" she lowered her voice to ask.

"Apprehensive. Jan rang while you were out there making your call. Your partner distracted the boys and started reading to them. Looks like she's having a good time. The boys love that book."

"She's in her element. I think she's crying out for grandchildren of her own to make an appearance, except her daughter is also a copper down in London."

"Ah, I take it that's not likely to happen for a while yet."

"I doubt it. Sorry, you were saying that you spoke with your in-laws. How did they take the news?"

"Oh, I couldn't tell Jan and Andrew over the phone. I've asked them to pop round to see us, they'll be here in a little while."

"What did you tell them?"

"That I had some news for them and left it at that."

Sally wiped the last of the dishes and moved on to the cutlery. Steve opened the drawer closest to her and nodded his appreciation.

"We'd better get this place spick and span for when they arrive, hadn't we? I also need to ask your permission to obtain your wife's medical and dental records," she said.

"God, that goes without saying."

FIVE MINUTES LATER, Jan and Andrew appeared at the back door. Steve unlocked it and welcomed them into the kitchen.

By this time, Lorne had finished reading the book, and everyone, including the kids, were in stiches.

"My, aren't you all having fun?" Jan said, a puzzled expression on her ageing face.

"Grandma, Granddad, we didn't know you were coming tonight," Haydon shouted and ran into Jan's arms, swiftly followed by Rory joining them in a group hug.

"It's an unexpected pleasure," Jan replied, her gaze flicking between Steve, Sally and Lorne. "What's going on?" she eventually asked.

"Why don't you see to the boys, Steve, and we'll have a chat with Jan and Andrew?" Sally suggested.

He seemed a tad uncomfortable when Jan's intimidating gaze dropped on him again. He nodded and smiled then marched the kids out of the room and upstairs.

"Who are you?" Jan demanded as soon as the door was closed behind him.

"Hi, sorry, I didn't want to make the introductions while the children were in the room. I'm DI Sally Parker, and this is DS Lorne Warner."

"The police. Why... no, it can't be... do you have news about our daughter?" Her voice faltered several times.

Sally gestured to the sofa. "Why don't you take a seat?"

Jan and her husband moved in front of the sofa and lowered themselves in slow motion while staring at Sally.

"You've found her, haven't you?" Jan murmured.

"We think so. There are dozens of tests that need to be carried out yet, before a formal identification can be announced, but Steve has confirmed that certain items which were found with the remains we discovered, belonged to Gail."

Jan immediately broke down and cried. Her husband flung an arm around her shoulders and pulled her into his chest.

"My God, we'd lost all hope of... where?" Andrew asked.

"In Cavendish Lake. You're probably aware that the lake has been dry for a few days due to the drought. Well, what appears to be your daughter's remains were found near what would be the centre of the lake."

Jan's head rose, and she stared at Sally open-mouthed. Finally, she asked, "Her remains? How were they found?"

Sally sighed. "In a hessian sack."

Jan sobbed and curled into her husband once more. It took several long moments for her to settle down and ask the next question. "What makes you think it's her? After all this time, how can you be so sure?"

"There were certain items found in the sack. I have photos of them if you'd like to take a look?" Sally removed her phone and stepped towards the sofa.

At first Jan turned away, but then, after a moment's pause, she regarded the images Sally showed her.

"Yes, that's her belt buckle, I'd know it anywhere. Her brother gave it to her when they were both in their teens. It might even have been when she was eighteen."

"We believe there aren't many in circulation, can you confirm that?"

"Yes, I can confirm that it was specially commissioned for Gail." She sobbed again.

"Do you know how she died?" Andrew asked, his voice catching in his throat.

"Not yet. It's going to be hard to establish because of various factors. That's why the lab will be running dozens and dozens of tests over the coming weeks."

"Are you telling us that there's nothing left of her, only bones?" Andrew asked. "Or is that a stupid question after all this time?"

"Not at all, there are no stupid questions in a case like

this. I'm afraid we're dealing with the skeletal remains of your daughter."

Andrew shuddered and squeezed his wife harder as the tears flowed faster.

Suddenly, Jan sat upright, and her gaze darted between Sally, Lorne and her husband. "Why has Steve taken this so well? He was smiling and joking when we arrived."

"It was all a show for the kids' sake," Sally felt the need to stick up for the woman's son-in-law.

"Was it? Over the years he has shown very little in the way of emotion about my daughter's disappearance."

Sally inclined her head. "What are you suggesting? That Steve is possibly behind your daughter's death?"

"Now, Jan, what have I told you about letting that imagination of yours run away with you?" Andrew stated.

"I'm not, it's been there all along, you ask Phil. We've had many a conversation over the years. Why do you think he's been off with him?"

Andrew tutted and shook his head. "Phil has always been jealous of their relationship, always wanted what Gail and Steve had but has never managed to achieve it for himself."

Sally cleared her throat to interrupt their conversation. "Sorry, who is Phil?"

"Our son," Jan and Andrew said in unison.

"Ah, that makes sense. I have to say something, if you don't mind. I'm getting the impression you don't trust Steve, and yet, since we arrived, he's had nothing but good things to say about you."

Jan inhaled a breath that inflated her chest. She clung tighter to her husband's hand. "We needed to put on a front for the children's sake. If we had shown any animosity or anger towards Steve, then he might have put his foot down and refused us access to Haydon and Rory. You hear about it all the time in the news; once a family breaks down, it's usually the grandparents who suffer. We refused to allow that to happen. It was a genuine struggle at times to bury my true feelings, especially when I was alone with him. The image of him throttling my daughter or stabbing her with a kitchen knife was never far from my mind whilst speaking to him. Truth be told, I cringe, he makes my skin crawl, but I've pushed through the barriers over the years with one main aim, to try and get to the truth."

"The truth about how he killed your daughter?"

She nodded. "Yes."

Sally turned to Lorne, amazed by the revelation. Lorne looked equally mystified.

"I think we need to discuss this further, but elsewhere, not here, not in Steve's home. Can you make an excuse to leave and we'll follow you back to your house? How does that sound?"

"I can say I was distraught by the news, which isn't a lie, and Andrew insisted we go home, if you like?"

"Great idea. Want me to tell him?" Sally asked.

"If you wouldn't mind. Do you need our address?"

"Give it to DS Warner. I'll nip up and let Steve know that we're leaving and we'll be with you shortly. You're not far away, are you?"

"No, about seven minutes' drive."

With her heart pumping her blood around her body wildly, Sally ventured upstairs where she found Steve, the doting father, bathing his children. "Hi, sorry to interrupt. We're going to pop off now."

He left the children and walked into the hallway. He leaned against the wall so he could still watch over them in the bath. "How did it go with Jan and Andrew?"

"She's distraught. I've told them to go home. I thought it would be better for all concerned, taking into account the emotions you're dealing with after hearing the news today."

"Thank you. Will you tell them I'll give them a call later, once the boys are in bed?"

"Of course. If I were you, I'd leave it a day or two, let things settle a little, for all of you."

"Okay. Give them my best wishes, and thank you, to you and your partner, for being so kind to me and my children, Inspector."

"It's been our pleasure. You have a wonderful family. Gail would have been proud to see the way you have brought up her children." She was testing him with her words.

His eyes welled up with tears. "Thank you. I've done my very best for them since she went missing. It's been a real struggle at times, but we've come through it, but only with Jan and Andrew's help."

"They seem nice people, you all do. We'll be in touch again soon. Take care."

"Thank you for dealing with our case, Inspector. I know you won't let us down." He glanced back at his kids splashing about in the bath. "They need answers as well as us."

"And we'll find them, don't worry. My team are experts at leaving no stone unturned, you have my guarantee."

"I believe you and have every faith in your ability."

*There, he didn't even flinch, that tells me a lot. I think Jan is wrong, but it'll be interesting to see what she has to say on the subject.*

Sally returned to the kitchen. Jan and Andrew were standing by the back door.

"All's good. He told me to send you his best wishes and that he will ring you in a day or two. That was my suggestion."

"We'll see about that. Hopefully you'll have enough on him to put him away before then," Jan bit back.

"Maybe. We'll leave by the front door and follow you home."

They walked out of the back door and left Sally and Lorne staring at each other.

"Let's talk it over in the car," Sally said.

Lorne nodded and led the way back through the house to the front door. Sally closed it gently behind her and pressed the key fob to unlock the car.

She sat in the driver's seat and tipped her head back. "Jesus… I'm not sure if I'm prepared for what is ahead of us."

"We can't leave it there, Sal. We need to find out what her parents have to say. Bugger what the time is."

"I know. I wasn't thinking about the time of day. My mind is shot. This revelation has blown it into a thousand pieces."

Lorne rubbed her arm. "Stick with it. Want me to ring Tony and Simon, warn them we're going to be late? Oops, we're already later than normal."

"Tell them we'll be home in a couple of hours, if not sooner."

# CHAPTER 6

Sally drew up outside a detached house on the outskirts of the next village. The garden at the front was immaculately tended, even if the lawn was scorched by the lack of rain in recent months. It was obvious either Jan and Andrew were green-fingered enough to care about their plants and the display on view to everyone passing.

Lorne let out a whistle. "Nice place."

"We're not here to admire their property," Sally snapped and instantly apologised as she had done exactly the same earlier. "Sorry, I'm anxious about what we're going to come up against inside."

"It's okay, you're allowed to be. What's running through your mind?"

"I'm not sure. Steve seemed a decent enough chap to me. I think my perception of him is about to alter rapidly if Jan and Andrew have anything to do with it. Which, in the end, is only going to confuse the hell out of me."

"I get that. My advice would be, if you want to hear it, to take everything on board and we'll assess it together, over the weekend, if we have to. You know I'm not averse to doing that."

"I know. But you have a guest arriving, or have you forgotten Carol is showing up this evening?"

"Damn, for a split second, yes, I had. It doesn't matter, she'll understand. What's the betting she'll be pestering me, wanting to lend a hand?"

"Oh heck. I'm not sure how I feel about that." Sally laughed and jumped out of the car.

Andrew saw them arrive and was standing in the doorway, ready to welcome them. "Come in. Can I get you ladies a drink? I've sorted Jan and myself out with a brandy."

Sally smiled. "We're fine, don't worry about us. Should we remove our shoes?"

"Don't you dare. It hasn't rained in months, so it's not like the ground is dirty out there. Come through to the lounge."

They followed him across the tiled hallway and into the vast lounge that had an inglenook fireplace dominating the main wall and two large windows on either side. Jan was sitting on a large sofa, sipping her drink.

She gestured for them to sit in the sofa positioned at a right angle. "Would you like a drink?"

"Andrew has already offered, and we declined, thank you." Sally sat on one end of the sofa, and Lorne sat next to her with her notebook out, primed and ready for action.

Andrew dropped onto the cushion next to his wife, and they both took a large gulp of brandy.

"Right, where do we begin with this one?" Sally asked.

"It's up to you," Jan replied.

"Maybe you can tell us why you suspect Steve of killing your daughter?"

Jan pointed to her head and then placed a hand over her heart. "I know it in here but also feel it here."

"We're going to need more than that, Jan. What proof do you have?"

Jan and Andrew glanced at each other and shook their heads.

Jan's gaze returned to Sally, and she shrugged. "I haven't got any, not really. But you know what women's intuition is like, we should never dismiss it."

"Unfortunately, going on that alone won't help us get a conviction in court. We need solid evidence. Can you provide us with any?"

Jan's head lowered, and she stared at her drink. Sally switched her attention to Andrew and cocked an eyebrow.

He shook his head. "No, we can't."

"Then why remain friends with him? Only because of the children?"

"Yes. We couldn't lose them." Jan sniffled. "If I lost contact with them, I would kill myself. It's surprising what you're prepared to do when the only connection to your daughter is in jeopardy."

"I can't pretend to know what you're going through, or the trauma you've had to contend with the past five years but, to me, that seems a little extreme. Thinking that he's killed your daughter and then eating at the same table with Steve, it simply doesn't ring true to me."

Jan went to open her mouth.

Sally silenced her with a raised hand. "I was going to add, but I don't have kids, so maybe that's why I'm struggling to get my head around it."

With that, a younger man entered the room, his bulging biceps on show and his taut thigh muscles straining his faded blue jeans. Sally immediately put a name to the stranger. *This must be Phil, Gail's brother.*

"Mum, Dad, what's going on? You're the police, aren't you? I can smell you... maybe I shouldn't say that."

"Now, Phil, don't you go kicking off, son," Jan said. "Just take a seat, and we'll tell you what's happened." She patted the cushion beside her.

He harumphed and threw himself onto the sofa, his thigh touching his mother's. "Go on then, tell me why you're here."

Apprehension, maybe even nervousness descended with this man's presence, for some reason, and Sally glanced at Lorne for help. She took over the reins.

"We've shared some grave news with your parents about your sister."

"What news? Have you found her? Is she alive? Grave news, no, that can only mean one thing." Phil reached for his mother's spare hand, the one not suffocating her glass of brandy.

"Sadly, yes. Remains were found a few days ago. We're waiting for confirmation that it is your sister, but we have reason to believe it is her," Lorne told him.

"How can you say that? What's she on about, Mum? Either it is her or it isn't."

"There were a few items found in the sack along with Gail's... body," Jan informed him.

"What items? Come on, tell me."

Sally winced at the agitation in his tone and had a nasty feeling that things were about to deteriorate quickly. She left her seat and showed him the image of the belt buckle. "Do you recognise it?"

"Yes. It's Gail's. I had it specifically made for her for her eighteenth birthday. You've found it?"

Sally returned to her seat and nodded. "In the sack, along with a few samples of clothing that appear to match other items in Gail's wardrobe."

"You've been to her home? *His* home? Does *he* know?"

Jan leaned over and whispered something in her son's ear. He slammed back in his chair and folded his arms.

"Yes. Your parents came to the house, explained they had some misgivings about Steve, and that's why we're here."

"Misgivings! Ha, that's one word for it," Phil hissed through thin, tight lips.

This man's arrogance made the hackles rise on the back of Sally's neck. "And what would you call it?"

"Some detectives you are… You were at his house, and you walked away without even dragging his arse in for questioning."

"We questioned him at the house." Sally paused and sucked in a calming breath. "And I have to admit that I didn't read anything untoward in his demeanour or the answers he gave us. It wasn't until your parents showed up at the house and Steve left the room that alarm bells rang. However, neither your mother nor your father has given us valid proof that Steve's conduct should be brought into question. Are you going to tell us differently?"

He grumbled something indecipherable, and his shoulders hunched up to cover his ears. "Don't think you can tie us into knots. I've dealt with your sort before. Always showing off, think you're better with the spoken word than the likes of me, who is out there, working his fingers to the bone, grafting, doing a decent day's work for a pittance of a wage."

Sally frowned. "I'm sorry, if that's what you believe. All I've tried to do is explain the situation to you in simple terms, nothing bamboozling about it, in my opinion." Sally turned to Lorne to get verification.

Lorne nodded.

"Why won't you take our word?" Jan asked again.

Sally raised her upturned hands. "I've already pointed out that if you can't give us proof, then the CPS—sorry, the Crown Prosecution Service—will laugh at us."

"How did she die?" Phil demanded.

"Again, as I told your parents, we're not likely to know

that until dozens of tests are carried out by the pathologist. Once a body has been submerged in water, it can hinder the professionals doing their utmost to identify the remains or cause of death. At least now, with your family recognising the belt buckle, it gives us a head start and other DNA can be sought."

"Meaning what?" Phil challenged.

"From the bones, plus the dental records can be obtained and compared to the remains."

He glanced at his mother and sighed. "I guess we're going to have to sit tight a little while longer, Ma."

Jan patted one of his huge thighs. "We're going to need patience, Phil."

"All right, I get that, but what I want to know is, what your next step is going to be. I get the impression that you're not going to believe anything we have to say about *him*. It seems to me that you've made up your mind already about him and us. Have you?"

"Not at all. Not wishing to harp on about it but, without any physical evidence, our job is going to be a hundred times harder. I'm sure you can appreciate that, can't you?"

"Yes, we can," Jan replied. She nudged her son's knee with her own.

"Why don't we leave things there for now? Give you time to think about it over the weekend? You can get back to me on Monday if you think of anything that I might need to delve into."

The three family members glanced at each other and shrugged.

"If this isn't your way of backing out of solving the case," Phil stated.

"It isn't," Sally confirmed. "DS Warner and I will meet up over the weekend and go over the case, see if the previous officer in charge of the investigation missed anything obvious and go from there. I'm going to need you to trust us. We've never let a family down yet, not since the Cold Case Team was originally set up."

Jan sipped at her drink and then said, "Please, don't let us down. The truth is out there. We're anxious to know what it is and how our daughter lost her life."

"If it's there, we'll find it, I promise."

Sally and Lorne rose from their seats, and Andrew showed them to the door.

"Please forgive my son's behaviour. They were extremely close, him and Gail. I don't think he's ever got over the shock of her going missing, and now that you think you've discovered her body, his emotions are in a total spin, just like ours."

"You don't have to apologise. We can't pretend to know what this news must have meant to you. All I can do at this stage is give you the assurance that we're going to do our absolute best to uncover the truth, no matter how long it takes."

"By that, you mean it could take days or weeks?"

Sally smiled. "Blimey, I'm hopeful it's the former, however, I have to be honest with you and ask you to be prepared and also to be patient. We'll be in touch as soon as we know anything, I swear."

"Then that's good enough for me."

Sally and Lorne left the house, and he closed the door gently behind them.

"Another tough one. I thought the son was going to be over-the-top confrontational for a minute there," Lorne said.

They reached the car.

Sally's gaze drifted back to the house. "I don't mind admitting that he intimidated me a little back there. Thanks for stepping in and taking over the questioning for a few minutes."

"I could tell you were struggling, but you regained your

composure quickly and ploughed on, that's the main thing, Sal. Are we calling it a day now?" Lorne pointed at the clock on the dashboard. It was just gone six-thirty.

"We might as well. Want me to go straight home, or do we need to go back to the station to pick your car up?"

"No, I don't need it for anything. Tony can drop me in to fetch it in the morning."

"If you're sure. I'm going to ring Jordan on the way back, see how he got on at the prison."

"It'll be interesting to find out. I thought he might have rung already to give us an update."

"Maybe his trip was delayed. We put a lot on his shoulders today, asking him to have a word with a second inmate while he was out that way."

They dropped into their seats.

Sally set off and then called Jordan. "Hi, it's me. Where are you?"

"Umm... I've not long left the prison, boss. On my way back to the station now."

"We're heading home, so if your intention was to see me, don't bother. How did you get on?"

"Let's just say I've had an interesting afternoon."

"In what respect?"

He hesitated and then sighed. "I think I should fill you in personally, boss. What if I drop by your house on the way home?"

"Sounds ominous. Do you know the address?"

"Can you remind me?"

Sally furnished him with the details. "How long do you reckon you'll be?"

"A good thirty minutes, possibly a little longer. Will that inconvenience you?"

"Not at all. See you soon. Oh, and Jordan..."

"Yes, boss."

"Are you sure you're okay?" Sally thought he sounded strange, and overwhelming guilt rattled through her for sending him out there alone. She should have insisted he took another member of the team.

"I'm fine. I'll fill you in soon."

"Drive carefully," Sally said then ended the call.

"He didn't sound okay to me," Lorne voiced, concerned.

"I was thinking the same. I'll find out soon enough. Let's get home and deal with what lies ahead when it comes our way."

As it was, Tony and Carol were both at Sally's house, having a sociable drink with Simon, when they arrived.

Lorne launched herself into Carol's outstretched arms, and they both needed to wipe away a few tears.

"It's wonderful to see you again. Did you have a good trip?" Lorne asked.

"Apart from witnessing an accident on one of the minor roads, close to here at the end of my journey, nothing major, no lives lost, but it held the traffic up for around half an hour until the tow trucks came to take the vehicles away. You're looking well, Lorne, Norfolk obviously suits you, or is it being back on the force that's made the difference?"

Lorne grinned. "I think probably the latter. I love working alongside Sally."

"Creep!" Tony flung at her, and they all laughed.

"You always did get on well together, from what I can remember of the conversations we used to have, Lorne."

"Well, it would be nice if someone offered us a drink. It's been a fraught day, hasn't it, partner?" Sally asked.

Lorne rolled her eyes to the ceiling. "It has that, and it's not finished yet."

As if on cue, the doorbell rang.

Sally went to answer the door. "My God, what happened?"

Jordan's right eye was a patchwork of blue, purple and grey. She pulled him into the hallway and shouted for Lorne to join them. "Lorne, have you got a minute?"

Lorne appeared and closed the door to the kitchen behind her. "Jesus, Jordan. What the fuck happened to you?"

"No, wait. Come through to the lounge. Can I get you a stiff drink, Jordan?" Sally latched on to his forearm and dragged him through the hallway and into the lounge. She deposited him in the best seat in the house and dashed over to pour the young officer a whisky.

"Only a snifter, boss. The last thing I need to obtain today is a bunch of points on my licence."

"All right, just a small one, to ease the pain."

"Or the humiliation," he mumbled.

Sally returned with the crystal tumbler and held it out to him. Jordan took it, his hand shaking uncontrollably.

"Look at the state of you," Sally said. "Why didn't you call for assistance? One of us would have come over and given you a lift back."

"No. It's too dangerous for either of you to go out there. Women should never set foot in that place, ever."

"I've visited it plenty of times over the years and never had a problem. What's going on, Jordan?" Sally had a sneaky suspicion that this had something to do with her ex-husband, Daryl.

Jordan sipped at his drink while Sally caught Lorne's attention and mouthed, "Daryl did this!"

Lorne sighed. "You can't know that," she mouthed in return.

Sally held a clenched fist over her heart.

Lorne closed her eyes and shook her head.

"Is that better?" Sally asked.

"It's getting there, boss. Dulling the pain at least."

"Are you up to telling us what happened?" Sally sat next to him on the sofa and turned towards him, their knees nearly touching.

Lorne made herself comfortable in one of the armchairs. The apprehension etched into every crevice of her face.

"The interviews went swimmingly. They were what I would class as insightful, but when I was about to leave, things got lucky."

Sally inclined her head. "I don't understand, how, Jordan?"

"A guard was accompanying me back to the reception area when he was jumped. Two big goons beat him to the floor and kicked seven bells of shit out of him."

"Crap. Why?" Sally ran a hand through her hair, fearing her initial suspicion had been justified.

He paused then glanced up and looked Sally in the eye. "Then your ex appeared."

Sally gasped and slapped a hand over her mouth. "What the fuck did he want? No, was this to do with Daryl?"

"Yes. He pinned me up against the wall. I couldn't retaliate because by now, the other two goons were standing just behind him, glaring at me."

Sally placed her hand over his. "What happened next?"

"Somehow, he knew who I was. I peered over his shoulder at the guard; he was out cold. At that stage I didn't know if they'd killed him or not. I thought I was in the shit up to my neck, I can tell you."

"Fuck, I'm glad you're okay." Sally smiled tautly. "I need to know what was said."

"He jabbed me in the stomach a few times and punched me in the face. Then told me to pass on a message to you."

Sally's stomach flipped over several times, and her heart

rate soared. She swallowed down the acid burning her throat and said, "Go on. I'm not going to like this, am I?"

"I doubt it. He told me that he was keeping an eye on you and that he misses you."

"What the fuck? The screwed-up piece of shit. How dare he take this out on you, how fucking dare he?"

"Sally, keep calm. We'll get him dealt with through the proper channels," Lorne insisted.

"He's got every frigging person in that shithole wrapped around his pinkie. Jordan, I'm so sorry he's done this to you."

Jordan shrugged. "It's over with, boss, I got out of there alive. No idea what condition the guard is in."

"How did you get away from him and his yobs?" Sally asked, her mind travelling at the speed of light.

"Once he'd put the fear of God into me and delivered his frigging message, he let me go. Warned me what would happen if I stopped and complained on the way out. So I collected my phone and car keys from reception and jumped in my car. I sat there for ages, contemplating whether I had done the right thing or not, leaving that guard there, but the more I considered the consequences, the more I felt sick to my stomach. Therefore, I got out of there, the coward that I am."

Sally furiously shook her head and gathered his free hand in her own. "Let's get one thing straight, you are *not* a coward. I will not accept that. You did what any normal person would do in your situation. You have nothing to be ashamed of, you hear me? I'm going to give the prison a call."

Jordan's head swivelled, and he stared at her. "You can't. They'll come after me, they told me they would."

"All right. Damn, but I need to know how the guard is."

Lorne clicked her fingers and shot out of her chair. "I know a way of finding out. I'll be right back." She tore out of the room and returned with Carol a few moments later.

"What the...? Are you all right, young man?" Carol asked from the doorway.

Carol and Lorne sat in the armchairs, and Carol held out a hand for Jordan to take.

Unsure, he hesitated.

Sally nudged him. "It's fine. Carol's one of the good guys."

He slipped his hand into Carol's, and she closed her eyes. After a few seconds she began rocking back and forth. "I see three men and the name Daryl is coming to me." Her eyes shot open, and her gaze fell on Sally. "It's your ex, he did this."

Sally nodded. "We know, Carol. What we need to find out is if the guard they attacked is okay?"

"Ah, let me see." She closed her eyes again. "I see Daryl standing over you. Two men were dealing with the guard. Ouch, they gave him a good beating with their fists and their boots. Wait... there's something else. There... yes, he's moving. His colleagues placed the three men in cuffs. I heard an alarm, and then the guard was helped to his feet by his colleagues. His concern lay with you. His colleagues told him that you had left the prison. He bent over and seemed relieved." She opened her eyes and smiled. "Is that it?"

Sally cocked an eyebrow. "Hardly, I think this is only the beginning. We need to have further discussions before you head back to London."

"I'm here for you, ladies. Why do you think I chose now to pay you a visit?"

Lorne laughed. "I knew there had to be a reason. We have a few unsolved cases that could do with your help, Carol."

"I'm aware. Shall we leave it this evening and pick up again in the morning?"

"Sounds good to me," Sally replied. "Are you sure you're okay, Jordan? Do you need to visit the hospital?"

"I'm fine. I was a bit shaken up, but now Carol has given us the news the guard is okay, all is good with me, boss."

"Do you want to go over how the two visits went? Anything urgent that you feel we need to look into, or can it wait until Monday?"

"Monday will do. I'll type up my notes over the weekend, have them ready for you first thing Monday."

"There's no need. Take the weekend to recuperate. We'll have a meeting when we all get into work. I can't apologise enough for what you've been through, Jordan."

"It's not your fault, boss. I have to say, you're well rid of that dickhead."

Sally smiled. "Yep, I came to that conclusion all by myself a few years ago. You get off, try and enjoy your weekend."

He downed the rest of his amber liquid and put the glass on the coffee table. "Have a good one, all. Thanks for the drink, boss."

"It's the least I could do. Take care. Keep alert during your drive home, you hear me?"

"Don't worry about me, I'll be fine. I'll show myself out." He waved and left the room.

"Bloody Daryl, I have to get something done about him. He continues to blight my life. What if that had been you at the prison today, Lorne? It could have been."

"Don't even go there. We're going to need to have a serious think about what we can do about him. Maybe call on some experts in the field of dealing with manipulative or out-of-control prisoners. How the heck is he allowed to get away with using the intimidating tactics he's used so far? The man is pure evil."

Carol sighed. "He's got the governor in his pocket. He might come across as a nice man to you, but he's another devious individual you need to be cautious about."

The news came as an utter shock to Sally. She had always

got on well with Governor Ward. Could Carol be right? "I guess you never really know someone until something like this occurs."

"Exactly. I'm tired now, sorry, ladies. I'm not as young as I used to be. All this drama takes its toll on me these days. It's all very draining, but I'm delighted to have been of some use to you."

"It's been a long day for us, too. Why don't we meet up in the morning for coffee, say around eleven?" Sally suggested. "Wait, that's too near lunchtime, you might as well come for lunch instead."

Lorne and Carol nodded.

"Sounds good to me," Lorne replied.

"That's settled then. We can have a conflab in here while the two fellas mess about in the kitchen, knocking up some delicious food for us to sample."

Carol jerked her thumb in Sally's direction. "Who is she trying to kid, in Tony's case?"

"Hey, you. He's got considerably better since we left London. It must be all the fresh air up here." Lorne chortled.

"Not the words I'd ever thought I'd hear coming from your lips, Lorne."

"Shocker, right? Come on, let's go. That is, if you're sure you're all right, Sally?"

"I'm fine. It's Jordan I feel sorry for. He was only carrying out instructions and he got clobbered for it. Poor man."

"He's resilient. He'll be fine. Nothing a few more glasses of whisky won't cure this evening."

"Everything all right?" Tony asked. He hooked an arm around Lorne and pulled her in for a kiss.

"It's fine. I'll tell you later. Any news on the dinner front, or do I need to come up with something when I get in?"

"No, it's all in hand. There, that's shocked you, hasn't it? I've made a curry that will blow your socks off."

Lorne winced. "Carol hates a hot curry."

"Damn, I forgot. I can knock you up a small pizza, if you'd rather have one, Carol?"

"Hush now, let's get home and then I'll decide. If I hang around here much longer, you're going to need to carry me home. I'm dead on my feet."

"We'll leave you to it and see you in the morning, Sally." Lorne kissed her on the cheek and whispered, "Enjoy your evening. Stop that mind of yours working overtime."

Sally pulled back and smiled. "Have a good evening, see you in the morning. Thanks for your help, Carol. Make sure you rest up this evening."

"I'll be having dinner and getting myself straight off to bed, I can tell you."

Lorne was right. Simon had cooked up a beautiful salmon and broccoli quiche and served it with salad, but halfway through the meal, Sally drifted off when her mind recapped the case and how they should proceed.

"I said... hey, are you even listening to me?"

Sally bit her lip. "I'm sorry, no." She bashed her temple with her clenched fist a few times. "Too much going on up here. Forgive me?"

She could tell by his expression that he was hurt. A smile appeared on his handsome face, and all was well again. "All right, but only if you finish off your quiche."

"Goes without saying."

"Want to discuss it or leave it for tonight? It might be better talking things over. You know what you're like, information tends to fester, and then you end up staring into the darkness all night."

"No, let's leave it for now. You can help me take my mind off things by telling me how your day has been."

He let out a full belly laugh. "Umm... that's what I was in the process of doing. It didn't stop you from drifting off before, so what makes you think it will be different this time around?"

"Ouch... I'm such a poor excuse for a wife."

"You're not. Stop putting yourself down unnecessarily. Finish your meal, and we'll retire to the lounge and go over the investigation there, deal?"

She smiled and chomped down on a mouthful of lettuce, laced with his special sumptuous honey and mustard dressing. The meal was excellent, and she felt ashamed that she hadn't appreciated how good the first half had been when she'd eaten it. "To make up for it, I'll do the dishes."

He stared at her, and then his mouth dropped open.

"What have I said now?" she asked.

"Nothing. Are you sure you'll be able to manage to wash up two plates and the relative cutlery?"

She picked up the serviette and threw it at him. "Stop teasing me."

"Okay."

They completed the meal, then Sally washed the dishes. They took their topped-up glasses of wine into the lounge and flopped onto the sofa with Dex at their feet. Sally gave her treasured dog a belly rub.

"I never thought I'd see the day when I was envious of a bloody dog." Simon gave her a toothy grin.

"Something for you to look forward to when we go to bed."

"Indeed." He waggled his eyebrows. "Now, tell me what's going on with your investigation."

Sally spent the next five minutes bringing him up to speed.

His expression was one of thoughtfulness once she'd revealed all the facts. "And what is your police gut telling you?"

"That Steve is innocent."

"Do you know how his wife went missing?"

"She'd been to the gym and was walking home, except she never made it."

"Do you reckon someone was stalking her?"

Sally shrugged. "Either that or she was damned unlucky and took someone's fancy. I don't have a clue how we're going to find out the motive behind her disappearance after all these years. Whoever is guilty of abducting her could, or should I say *is*, probably long gone by now."

"Hey, that's not like you, putting obstacles in the way. You need to reassess, go back to the basics and start all over again. Did she go to the gym by herself that night or with friends?"

She stared at him sheepishly. "I never got around to asking either the husband or the parents that question."

"All is not lost. Hey, and don't forget you have Carol here to help you. Lorne swears by her abilities. All right, she might be a bit rusty, but surely people never lose the knack of contacting the dead once it's embedded in them, do they?"

"I'm not sure. They're coming for lunch tomorrow... oops, maybe I should have mentioned that snippet of information sooner."

He pulled her close and kissed the top of her head. "You had your mind elsewhere. What about Jordan? Are you going to tell me what happened to him?"

Sally stretched out her neck and rolled her head in a full circle to ease out the knots of tension that were accumulating. "He was sent on a mission to Norwich Prison today, on a different case that he and Lorne were dealing with for me. Well, when the news broke about Jack's dad, and I requested Lorne's services to be my partner, Jordan told me he was up to going out to the prison alone." She shuddered, and Simon squeezed her shoulders tighter.

"Go on. Tell me."

"I dread to think what the outcome may have been if Lorne had gone with him."

"What happened to Jordan? Did he get attacked?"

"Yes, by Daryl and a couple of his goons. Correction, he lumped Jordan while his goons literally knocked seven bells of shit out of the guard who was accompanying Jordan back to the reception."

"Damn, was he all right?"

"For now. I can't help wondering what state Lorne would have been in if she had shown up at the prison today, with Jordan, instead of teaming up with me."

"You can't even consider that. She wasn't there, so there's no point punishing yourself about it, Sal. No wonder you were distracted throughout dinner. Did Daryl say anything to Jordan?"

"He told him to pass on a message that he was watching me and that he missed me."

Simon released his hold on her and sat forward on the edge of the sofa. "What the…? He can't intimidate you like this. For a start, I won't allow it, but aren't there rules in place? Can't he get done? Wait a minute, aren't there strict conducts they have to adhere to inside? How were they able to get to Jordan?"

"Carol told us not to trust the governor. What if he's got him and the screws in his pocket, allowing him to move about the prison at will?"

"That's a serious allegation, love."

"Don't I know it? You tell me what the alternative is, because I can't for the life of me think of one." The emotion that had wracked her body for the past couple of hours, since Jordan had revealed the truth, suddenly overwhelmed her. She buried her head in her hands and broke down.

"Oh God, I hate seeing you in such a state. We can't allow him to get away with this."

"I just need to get it out of my system, I'm sorry. I thought I was over him, I mean I am, but I suppose I'm never going to be rid of him, am I?"

"We'll soon see about that. I won't rest until he's punished for putting you through this shit, it shouldn't be allowed to happen."

She kissed him on the cheek and smiled through her tears. "My hero. Maybe all we should do is ignore him. That's bound to wind him up, not getting a reaction from us."

"I'll have a word with a friend of mine, a criminal barrister, see what he has to say about the situation. We have a right to our freedom. Just because he gave up his rights by breaking the law, it doesn't mean to say he can pop up now and again to remind us that he's still around. Maybe we can get him moved to a different prison."

"I'm in need of some fresh air. Fancy taking Dex for a stroll down by the river?"

Dex raised his head after earwigging their conversation and hearing the word *river*, his favourite place, mentioned.

"Why not? I'll get rid of the glasses and join you in the hallway."

They shared a quick kiss and left the room. Dex bounced around once she unhooked his lead from the coatrack.

"Sit, be good, you're like a jumping bean when you're all excited."

A glass smashed in the kitchen. Sally clutched Dex's lead and rushed to the doorway. "Are you all right?"

"It slipped out of my hand, no damage done. Sorry to scare you."

"It can be replaced, as long as you're all right. Are you?"

He batted away her concern with a swipe of his hand. "I'll be there in a tick."

Sally returned to put her trainers on and then riffled through the coats to find her waterproof jacket, just in case they got caught in one of the showers the weatherman had been predicting was imminent to ease the drought.

Simon appeared a few seconds later and slipped on his trainers. "Fit to go?"

"Yes, looking forward to it."

# CHAPTER 7

As arranged, Lorne, Carol and Tony showed up at the house at eleven the following morning. Sally, instead of feeling chilled, revealed that her stomach had been in knots all through the night.

"Mine, too," Lorne admitted. "I'm sensing we're close, we just need to find a few pieces of the missing puzzle to steer us in the right direction."

"And that's where you're hoping I will come in, is it?" Carol pitched in.

Sally and Lorne nodded.

"Let's get you fixed up with a drink first. What would you like?" Sally asked.

"Coffee, white with one for me, if you wouldn't mind."

Simon cleared his throat. "I'll make them, and then Tony can help me set up the barbecue. What time shall we eat? About twelve-thirty to one?"

Sally conferred with Lorne and Carol to check if the time was suitable, and then they went through to the dining room.

"Will this do?"

"Yes, this is pretty much the perfect environment, not too bright in here, although I might ask you if we can close the curtains." Carol scanned the room. "The spirits tend to prefer to show themselves when the room is dull, no rays of sunshine targeting the room."

Sally closed the pair of curtains on the right, and Lorne did the same with the other window.

Then Sally nipped out of the room. She returned, coffees in hand, to find Carol sitting at the table, her eyes closed, summoning the spirits. Sally's mouth twisted as she gave Lorne her cup.

Lorne held up her crossed fingers and then took a sip of coffee.

They sat around the table, on either side of Carol, and watched her go through the motions before she came to an abrupt halt. Sally's gaze met Lorne's, and then they turned their attention to Carol once more.

She whispered, "Yes, I hear you. Can you tell me your name?"

"You haven't told her, have you?" Sally mouthed at Lorne.

"Definitely not," Lorne mouthed in return.

"Gloria…? Gillian…? Am I getting closer…? I am? What is it sweetheart? Come forward and speak with us. Lorne and Sally won't harm you, none of us will, we're here to help set you free."

Sally wondered if they should form a ring and be holding hands, like they showed on TV, but as Carol hadn't suggested it, she abruptly dismissed the idea.

"Gail, is that what you're telling me? It's the only G I know from the characters in Coronation Street… Gail, yes, it suits you. Come forward, love, don't be shy, you're amongst friends here." Carol opened her eyes and whispered, "She's here, she's a little reluctant to speak with me. I'm not going to push her, she needs to do it in her own time."

"That's fine, Carol. How does she seem to you?" Sally looked at Lorne who was chuckling. "What am I supposed to ask? I know, it wasn't the smartest question to come out of my mouth."

"Hush now, Lorne, don't be so harsh," Carol said. "Sally is all new to this, you have years of experience behind you."

"Sorry. Consider my wrist slapped," Lorne said, her smile slipping.

Carol closed her eyes again and called out, "Gail, are you still with us?"

"Is she?" Sally asked.

Carol opened her eyes and shook her head. "She's gone… for now. They have a tendency to hang around in the background. Why don't we try and piece things together? She might feel the need to have her presence felt if we say something she doesn't agree with."

"I'm fine with that," Sally replied. "Where do we start?"

"One thing that has worked well with the spirits I've tried to communicate with over the years is me talking about their family. We could give that a try," Lorne suggested.

Carol pointed. "So it has. Let's do it. Does she have a husband?"

"Yes, Steve. He seems a nice enough chap, although Gail's mother and father, and her brother come to that, would be inclined to disagree with me."

Carol's head remained still, but her gaze travelled the perimeter of the room. "Nothing. Does she have children?"

Lorne smiled. "That's sure to do the trick. Sally and I met the two dear souls yesterday, Haydon and Rory."

Carol closed her eyes and sat upright. "Ah, you'd like to know all about them, wouldn't you, sweetheart? Well, if Lorne says they're dear souls then they must be perfect angels."

"They were. They have excellent manners and they clearly love their father very much."

"That news is such a relief to her. The boys were her absolute world. She was with them day and night. Adored them, never found it a chore to be with them. If it hadn't been for the excess pounds she was left carrying after Rory came along, she would never have entertained going to the gym that night," Carol said, her voice breaking with emotion.

"Can she tell us what happened?" Sally probed, making sure that she avoided asking how Gail had actually died.

Carol's eyes lit up, and she said, "Yes, dear. If you can… in your own time… yes, we all appreciate how tough this must be for you… your family needs justice to be served. That's why we're here… to help you achieve just that. Trust us, we're all good people."

Carol paused for a few moments longer, enough time to think that Gail's spirit had drifted away again. However, that wasn't the case.

"Someone jumped you from behind, you didn't see who it was… they bundled you into the backseat of a car and put a sack over your head."

"Were you conscious?" asked Sally, her slippery hands wringing together.

"Yes. She could hear them talking," Carol confirmed.

"How many were there?" Sally shuffled forward to the edge of the dining chair and cast an eye in Lorne's direction. Her partner was avoiding eye contact, her gaze locked on to the fruit bowl in the middle of the table. "Lorne, are you all right?" Sally asked. She nudged her knee under the table.

"Huh… oh yes, I'm fine. I've been here so many times before," Lorne whispered in return.

*What is that supposed to mean? To tamp down my enthusiasm in case things go belly up or what?*

Carol fell silent.

"How many, Carol?" Sally prompted.

"I don't know, she's gone. Sometimes they use so much energy to come here that it zaps their strength."

Sally glanced at Lorne who was displaying a 'told you so' kind of expression.

"Oh well, maybe she'll hang around with us while her batteries recharge."

"I wouldn't count on it," Lorne stated, tutting.

"What's got into you, Lorne?" Carol demanded. "I've never seen you so dejected before. Yes, we've had a few instances similar to this over the years, but the information certain spirits have provided has been beneficial to a good few of your cases, you have to admit that, don't you?"

"Sometimes. There has always been the odd occasion when a killer has gone free because the spirit refused to cooperate halfway through 'the interview'," Lorne said.

"I can tell I'm not going to win this argument. Do you want to call it a day now?" Carol grumbled.

"Would I be pushing my luck if I asked a few more questions, Carol?" Sally smiled and flipped open her notebook.

"Go ahead, Sally, nice to know my services are still useful to at least one of you."

"Well, this week alone we've been in touch with four other families, each of them searching for a loved one who was reported missing around five years ago. Is it worth a shot reaching out to see if anyone is around? Is that the correct terminology?" Sally asked with a shrug.

"Yes, let me see. Do you have any names?"

"Of the missing or the relatives?"

"Let's go with the relatives, shall we? I feel I have something I need to prove to you, Sally, and your partner over here."

Lorne jabbed a thumb at her chest. "Me? Not to me. I know what you're capable of, Carol."

"Then why are you so grouchy today?" Sally hissed.

"I'm not. All I'm doing is sitting here quietly."

Sally issued one of her don't-bullshit-a-bullshitter kind of looks and added one of Jack's personal favourite retorts, "Whatever. Right, first one up is Gary Porter."

Carol closed her eyes to concentrate and after several moments came out of her trance-like state and shook her head. "No, nothing, sorry. Next one?"

Sally flipped over the page and ran her finger down the notebook. "Eric Swallow?"

Carol dipped into another trance, and her reply came quicker this time. "Nothing. I'm so sorry to let you down like this, Sally. Maybe I'm more tired than I first thought."

"Would you rather call a halt to our meeting, there?" Sally asked.

Carol adamantly shook her head. "No, let's give it one last shot."

"How about Tim Benjamin?"

Carol's eyes drifted shut again. She fidgeted in her chair and then sat upright. "Yes, there's someone here. Come a little closer, dear. What's your name...? Tania, and he was your husband, was he? How did you die? Oh my, did someone push you into the water...? They abducted you? Do you know who it was? Oh heck, and then she was gone. I'm sorry but as you probably gathered, Tania is no longer with us. She had a watery grave. Swept out to sea, I believe. Someone picked her up, against her will. He bumped her over the head... umm... did unspeakable things to her and dumped her body in the estuary at Great Yarmouth. She told me she drifted for what seemed like months, ended up in the cold North Sea."

"This is great stuff, Carol. You're amazing, if all this is

true," Sally said with a slip of the tongue. "Can we go for one more?"

Carol pinched her temple with her fingers. "I'm exceptionally tired, but go on, what harm can it do?"

"Last one is Zach Connor—his daughter, no, I've said enough, sorry."

"Let me try and find her." After several fraught moments had passed, Carol's forehead collapsed onto her hand resting on the table.

"No more, that's enough for now," Lorne butted in. "Carol, are you all right? Can you hear me?" She shot out of her chair and lifted Carol's head.

"I'll get some water," Sally tore out of the room and into the kitchen.

"Is everything okay?" Simon asked.

Sally whizzed past him and filled the glass. "Slight emergency. Carol has fainted."

"Oh heck. Not again," Tony said. "Sometimes speaking with the spirits can totally drain her."

"I've got to get back in there. We shouldn't be too long. Hopefully, she'll be conscious again soon."

Sally opened the door of the dining room cautiously. "How is she?"

"She'll be fine. She's already told me off for making a fuss."

"Just give me two minutes' peace and I'll be okay," Carol muttered.

Sally placed the glass on the table and rubbed Carol's arm. "I'm sorry we pushed you so hard. This is a first for me, I didn't know what to expect."

Carol, seemingly still a bit dazed, righted herself and smiled. "It takes it out of me, every now and again. Now, don't you go apologising. All you're trying to do is help these poor families get the closure they deserve. I'll keep trying for you. I never give up."

"You need to rest, Carol. You've done enough for today." Lorne wrapped an arm around her dear friend's shoulder, but Carol shrugged it off.

"Now what have I told you about not making a fuss? Shh… someone is trying to communicate with me…. I'm still here. What do you need to tell me? Nicole or Nicola could it be?"

"Yes, Nicola," Sally confirmed. "Don't push yourself, Carol."

"I'm not. She's here. Nicola said she often visits her father, that's why he believes she is still alive. She doesn't want to see him devastated and thinks it would be better, for his health, he has a dodgy heart, if the truth was kept from him."

"We can make sure that happens, if she believes it's for the best," Sally replied. "How did she die?"

Carol paused once more and then opened her eyes. "Whoever took her buried her alive. She lasted for three days, fought hard to stay with us, but in the end, her body shut down."

"How sad." Sally's heart lurched. To know the young woman suffered in the final days of her life came as a severe blow, something she hadn't been expecting.

"She's at peace now. Watching over her father. She believes he's not long for this world and if you take away any hope he has of Nicola coming home, it'll have a detrimental effect."

"Please assure her we won't say anything to him."

Carol nodded and closed her eyes again, then whispered, "It was a game."

Sally's gaze sought out Lorne's, and they both frowned.

"What was?" Sally asked.

Carol swayed from side to side and then back and forth.

The motion made Sally feel sick and left her wondering how it would affect Carol after what had happened a few minutes before.

Lorne reached out a hand and placed it on top of Carol's. "Enough now. Let them go, Carol. That's not a request, that's an order."

Carol shook her head but sat still. "Gail. She's telling me it was some kind of game that went wrong and led to her death... wait, I have more news, about a Billy?"

Sally flicked through her notebook and found nothing.

"Billy Prather, Carol, is that the one?" Lorne said.

Carol took a few seconds before she confirmed. "Yes, that's the one. You didn't give me his name, did you? I'm a little puzzled by what I'm hearing. This woman is telling me she's a distant relative. She's telling me it's a vile miscarriage of justice, people need to start listening to him. He's telling the truth. His girlfriend is still alive, but she hasn't been well... Will you help her do the right thing...? Good, let's get this sorted."

"What was that all about?" Sally asked.

"His relative, his great aunt, is going to visit his girlfriend, Christine, and ease the fog that she is suffering from."

"I wish I knew what that meant," Sally replied.

"You will. All in good time. That's it from me. The last of the spirits have drifted away now." Carol took a large swig of water and then wrapped both her hands around the glass. "I'd say that was a good session, wouldn't you?"

"I hate to see how much these sessions are taking out of you these days, Carol. You keep pushing yourself too hard," Lorne chastised gently.

"Don't fuss. It was my pleasure. Now that the spirits have found me, it's not uncommon for them to try and make contact again. The families aren't the only ones who need closure, it means a lot to them as well. Once that has been achieved, they'll be able to go forward, on to their final resting place."

Sally inclined her head. "I never knew that."

"Well, you do now," Lorne said. "I think we all need a bit of sustenance after that undertaking. Let's see how far the boys have got with lunch without us being in their hair."

"What they've got left of it," Sally quipped.

## CHAPTER 8

After a whirlwind of adventures over the weekend, it was now back to reality with a bump. Sally brought the team together to go over what had happened on Friday before they broke up, but first she put Jordan in the spotlight and instructed him to tell his colleagues how the two interviews had gone down at the prison.

"Did one of them give you a black eye for asking an impertinent question, mate?" Stuart said.

Jordan glanced in Sally's direction, and she answered for him. "Unfortunately, that was the result of an ambush by my ex-husband. It's being dealt with by the authorities. Once again, I'm sorry you had to deal with that shit, Jordan, whilst carrying out important police business. It should never have been allowed."

"It's fine, boss. It looks worse than it is, I promise."

"Then proceed, if you will?"

"Eric Swallow was very open with me. Actually, after a while, both men were. And I have to say, I know we're told to guard what we feel about people in the system, however, I suspect both men have been cruelly treated."

"Again, maybe that's something we can look into further, when we have time to pursue matters," Sally suggested, remembering what Carol had mentioned over the weekend. "You were saying?"

"Eric Swallow, not that it is of consequence any longer, now we believe we've pinpointed who the victim really is… anyway, he has regrets for giving up on his children but thought it was for the best, knowing he had always had the urge to go on the rob."

"What? So he has no intention of reforming while he's on the inside?" Sally asked.

"Not from what I could tell, boss, no. I believe he's going to be what's known as a serial offender. He might complain about being locked up, but it's ultimately where he feels safe. He told me that if you keep your nose clean, it can be a safe environment."

Sally smiled and cocked an eyebrow. Jordan brushed a hand over his blackened eye.

"If you say so, Jordan. Now, how did things go with Prather?"

"That's a very sad case. He's always declared his innocence and told me that Falkirk kept him in the interview room for over twelve hours, trying to break him. In the end, exhausted and thirsty, he finally admitted that he had killed Christine."

"We can get him out of jail on that alone, can't we?" Lorne threw in. "It's against the rules to interview a suspect for that length of time, never mind that he wasn't given any meal or drink breaks during the interview. What an utter bastard that Falkirk was."

"Exactly, another case we're going to have to refer to the appeals board. The Crown Court will put things right, I'm sure. We have news on this case, but what I'm about to tell you remains in this room, we won't be able to publicly affirm any of it." Sally went on to tell the rest of the team about the session they'd held with Carol. She chuckled at the shocked faces staring back at her. "Now you can understand my need to keep a lid on it. Lorne has worked with Carol for years, solved several high-profile investigations with the psychic's help. Anyway, we have news on a couple of the other cases that we'll set aside for now. Jordan, you stick with the Prather case, let's see if we can get his conviction overturned on a technicality. Give me a shout if you need a hand."

"Will do, boss. I'll get back to it after the meeting."

"Good. Now we come to the victim, Gail. According to Carol, our psychic friend, there were two people involved in her abduction and ultimate murder. Carol informed us that there was some kind of game involved. Does anyone have any idea what that could be? I know I'm asking a lot here, but if we can come up with something feasible then maybe it will lead us to the killers."

The team all glanced at each other. A few shook their heads, and a couple of them shrugged.

"Off the cuff," Stuart announced, "what about some kind of dare? Or a bargain, something along the lines of, if you do this for me, I'll do this for you in return?"

Sally mulled over his proposal. "Possibly. Either way, we need to find out who's involved, and the only way we're going to do that is by questioning Gail's family and friends again, as well as her work colleagues. Lorne and I will do all the legwork. I need the rest of you to go through the files relating to the case and obtain the contact details of all those who were spoken to at the time Gail went missing. I have to say, I've been disappointed with the response we've received from the press conference. I'm wondering if it's worthwhile putting out an update, see if that brings in any news."

"Definitely worth a shot. Can you name the victim at this stage?" Lorne asked, clearly doubting her words.

"I don't feel inclined to, not until the identification has been officially confirmed. Yes, the belt buckle belonged to Gail, but it might have been stolen by the killers and…"

"What, dumped with another body?" Lorne added quickly.

Sally shrugged. "Your guess is as good as mine. Might even have been nicked by the killer and then, if there was a game involved and it turned sour, maybe the remains we've discovered will turn out to be the killer's."

Lorne's head jutted forward. "Seriously? That's like out of this universe kind of thinking."

Sally and Lorne laughed.

"Hey, if that's what's running through my mind then I have to go with it. One thing we do need to do right away is request her medical and dental records and arrange to get them sent over to the lab. Joanna, will you sort that out for me?" Sally asked.

Joanna smiled. "Of course."

"I have the details of the doctor and the dentist." Lorne flipped back through her notebook and jotted down the information on a spare sheet of paper which she handed to Joanna.

"Thanks, it shouldn't take me too long to get it organised."

"The sooner the better," Sally replied. "I'll be in my office, sorting out another press conference should anyone have any news for me." She fixed herself a coffee and entered her room. She picked up her phone and then sat behind her desk. "Georgia, it's Sally Parker, how are things going?"

"Oh, hi, I was about to ask you the same thing. Any luck with the last conference?"

"Not really. However, we believe we've identified the victim via the belt buckle but we're unsure if the remains belong to her or not. I know, that sounds like I'm talking a lot of nonsense."

"Not at all. What can I do for you, Sally?"

"I'm wondering if we can run an update, what do you reckon?"

"I'm up for it, if that's what you think is for the best."

"When can you arrange it for?"

"Let me get back to you in about half an hour. I think we have a slot this afternoon, it depends if the journalists are willing to play ball or not."

"You're amazing. We'd be lost without you to rely on."

"I haven't worked my magic yet, so don't praise me too soon."

"I'll leave it with you."

"Get back to you ASAP, I promise."

Sally ended the call and then took time out to mull over what to do next. While she was deep in thought, her mobile rang. Her heart raced when Jack's name appeared on the little screen. "Hey, I was going to ring you today at some point. How are things going down there?"

"Hi, we're doing okay, thanks. I didn't want you to forget me, so thought I'd get in touch."

"As if I could ever forget you."

"How's the case going?"

"So-so. I need to know how you're holding up first. Has the funeral been arranged yet?"

"Yes. It's tomorrow. Straight after that we'll be heading home. Thought I'd come back to work on Wednesday, if that's okay with you?"

"Sure, if you think you'll be up to it, Jack. Will you?"

"The truth is, I'm going out of my mind having all this time off. It's different when you've booked a holiday and made plans of what to do with your time, but being down here, planning out a funeral isn't my idea of fun, I can assure you."

"I bet. How's the family doing?"

"We're all eager to get back home now. It has been lovely catching up with distant relatives, but my cheeks are hurting from all the constant grimacing, I'm not used to it."

"Ah, you meant the cheeks on your face, I'm with you now."

Jack groaned. "You never stop, do you?"

"What? Hey, I wouldn't want to let you down. In all seriousness, I'm glad you're okay, partner. I was worried about you there for an itsy-bitsy moment."

"There's no need. How's my replacement been?"

"Fine. We've got on really well together, not that there was ever a doubt in my mind."

"Glad to hear it. I hope you're not tempted to make the situation a permanent one, are you?"

Sally paused, intentionally, aware how much it would piss her partner off. "Oh, sorry, I got distracted then for a moment. What was your question again?"

Jack heaved out a long sigh. "Not worth repeating. You're obviously too busy to speak with me. I'll go now and see you on Wednesday."

"Jack, I was teasing. Don't go off in a huff… for a change."

"You've got a bloody cheek. I don't get in moods, unlike some I could mention."

Her landline rang. "Saved by the bell. See you Wednesday."

"Have fun."

"I will. You, too, partner."

Sally answered the phone. It was Georgia. "That was quick. What time?"

"I've managed to arrange a lunchtime slot, at around twelve, if that's okay with you?"

"It's perfect. Thanks, I'll see you later, Georgia."

"My pleasure."

Sally spent the next hour or so answering urgent emails

until Joanna knocked on the door and poked her head into the room.

"Hey, what's up?" Sally asked.

"Nothing, everything is fine. Just to let you know that I've called the surgery and the dentist's and given them details of where to send the medical records of Gail Morton."

"Great news. Did they say how long that is likely to take them?"

"Hopefully, time permitting, should be by the end of the day."

"At least things are moving in the right direction, at last. I've got a few more emails to sift through then I'll come and join you. Tell Lorne I have arranged a conference for midday. How's she doing, getting in touch with everyone on the list we need to speak to?"

"She's busy working her way through it now."

"We can venture out after lunch."

"I'll pass the message on to her, boss. Do you need anything else from me?"

"Nope, all clear at the moment. Thanks, Joanna."

THE CONFERENCE WENT OKAY; it was passable in Sally's opinion. Sadly, only one of the TV stations bothered to show up, along with around six journalists. Sally had hoped for more, but she'd come to expect the lack of response with investigations that were classed as cold cases. The public interest never matched that of an ongoing investigation. Sally could never understand why that was the case, but it was something, as a team, they would need to accept. She returned to the office to check on the team's progress in her absence.

"Right, round two of press conferences completed. How's it going here?"

"I have a list of people for us to interview, including best friends and workmates," Lorne replied.

"Come on then, I'm fed up with hanging around here today. Let's get out there and see what these people can tell us. Hopefully, someone will be able to fill us in on this game that went drastically wrong."

"I wouldn't hold my breath on that one," Lorne grumbled.

Sally collected her phone and handbag from her office and, by the time she returned, Lorne was waiting by the door for her.

"We'll be back soon, folks. The conference will be aired via the radio this afternoon but not on TV until this evening, so keep an eye on the phones. Let me know if anything significant comes in." She turned to face Lorne and said, "Right, who's first on that list of yours?"

On the way down the stairs, Lorne ran through the possible options.

"Okay, why don't we start with her best friends? From experience, they can usually fill in the gaps in someone's personal life, can't they?"

"That's what I'm thinking. The best two friends are sisters, and they both work at the same shop, as well, which makes life a lot easier, too."

"Excellent. Where are we heading?"

"Into Wymondham. They work in a small café called Quick Bite to Eat."

"Cute. Not heard of it."

"I haven't either."

THE CAFÉ WAS SITUATED among several other businesses ranging from sports shops to a clothing boutique. They parked in the main square and walked across the road. At this time of day, the café was busier than Sally had anticipated it would be. Although, there were a few empty tables left and Lorne grabbed the first one she came to.

"Will this do?"

"Yep, I suppose." Sally sat and glanced around. "I bet they won't be able to spare the time to have a chat."

"Don't be so negative. We can ask. It's not like we have to speak to them together. This place might run like a well-oiled machine and the manager might surprise us by allowing them to speak to us, even if it is approaching their busy time."

A young woman wearing a white lacy pinny over a black skirt and blouse arrived to take an order.

Sally flashed her warrant card. "Sorry, we're not here to eat. We're on official business and wondered if we could speak with either Lorraine or Linda Shaw."

"Oh, I see. Well, I'm Linda." She peered over her shoulder at the young woman preparing the coffee machine. "And that's my sister, Lorraine. I'm not sure what the boss will say about you showing up at this time of day."

"Is your boss around?"

"Sandra is in her office. She usually comes out in about half an hour to lend a hand when things get busy. I really think it would be better if we spoke to you later. Sorry, I should have asked, what's this about?"

"Gail Morton's disappearance."

Tears immediately sprang to Linda's eyes. "Oh God, have you found her? Is she alive? Please tell me she's alive, we've both missed her terribly."

"I'm sorry, I can't tell you that. We've recently discovered a body and we're awaiting the identification results from the lab."

Linda frowned. "I don't get it. Couldn't you tell it was her?"

"No, it's been five years, and the remains were found in a lake."

Shaking her head over and over, Linda tutted.

"Hey, sorry to interrupt," a man on the next table said. "I've been waiting ten minutes or more for my sandwich, it's usually quicker than this, and I have an appointment I need to keep in half an hour. Any chance you can chase it up for me?"

"Oh, yes, of course, sir. I'll do that for you now." She turned back to Sally and said, "I'm sorry, you can see how I'm fixed. I need to tend to the customers or I'll risk losing my job."

"What time do you finish?"

"At three-thirty, we both do. Can you come back then?"

Sally and Lorne rose from their seats.

"Shall we come back at three-thirty on the dot?" Sally asked.

"Just after, we have to get changed and do the cleaning before we leave. That'll take fifteen minutes or thereabouts."

"Three forty-five then. Don't worry, we have other people on our list to see in the meantime."

"Glad I won't be putting you out."

"You're not."

They left the café and jumped back in the car.

"Well, that was a waste of time," Sally said. "I suppose we were taking a risk showing up there at lunchtime."

"I did wonder. Where do you want to go now? To her employer?"

Sally inserted the key in the ignition, and the engine roared to life. "Which is where?"

"Not far from here. Robinson's Insurance."

"Ah, yes, I'd forgotten she was an insurance rep. It's just around the corner if my memory serves me right."

"I'm wondering if it might be wiser to leave the car here

and set off on foot."

"Good thinking. The traffic can be a nightmare around here during the day."

Sally switched off the engine and locked the car again, and within a few minutes they were standing inside the smart insurance office.

A woman in her forties, her specs slotted through her hair on the top of her head, approached them. "Hello, ladies, how may I help?"

Sally and Lorne produced their IDs.

"DI Sally Parker and DS Lorne Warner. We'd like a brief chat with your boss, if they're around."

"Ah, that would be Alan Victor. Yes, he's in his office. I'll let him know you're here."

"Thanks."

She scampered through the large room, weaving her way between the four desks, the occupants of which, two males and one female, stared at them.

Sally smiled. "Nothing serious, folks. I'm sure your boss will fill you in once we've gone."

The woman returned with a stockily built man dressed in a light-grey suit.

Sally and Lorne produced their IDs again.

"Is it possible to have a chat with you in private, Mr Victor?" Sally said.

"Regarding? Have I done something wrong?" he asked, puzzled.

"No, it's nothing like that. Please, it would be better if we spoke about this in private."

"Very well, come this way. Tricia, can you fix us some drinks?"

Lorne smiled and placed the order. "Two coffees, white with one sugar, thanks."

"I'll bring them in."

Alan showed them into his larger-than-average office. The first thing that caught Sally's eye was the huge fish tank in a mahogany cabinet along the main wall.

"Ah, I see you've noticed the fish. I find them very calming in the office. Every executive should have one... a tank."

Sally nodded and replied wistfully, "I used to have fish as a child, well, a lonely goldfish. I always felt sorry for it swimming round and round in circles all day long, but my parents refused to get me a posh tank."

"Yes, I've never been one for shoving a poor creature in one of those tiny bowls. No wonder goldfish don't tend to live long." He gestured for them to take a seat and sat in his executive chair.

"I never thought about it. Can't even remember how long Bob lasted. Silly name for a fish, I know. When he died, I desperately wanted to replace him, but my parents were adamant they didn't want another fish in the house. I suppose the cleaning out and feeding mostly fell on their shoulders. I kept forgetting to feed him."

Alan tutted. "They need constant care and attention. I've never agreed with children having pets because that's where the neglect comes into play."

*Consider me told. Pardon me for breathing.* "Anyway, let's change the subject before you start lecturing me on what food I should have fed him, it's bound to have been the wrong type."

"Ouch, sorry, did I come across as a know-it-all?" Alan cringed. "I'm just passionate about the little creatures. Tell me, why are you here?"

A knock on the door delayed Sally from answering his question.

Tricia entered carrying a tray and, after distributing the cups, she asked, "Can I get you anything else, sir?"

"That'll be all, thanks, Tricia. Close the door on your way out."

Sally waited until the woman had left and reached for her mug. "We're here to ask you some questions about a former colleague of yours."

Alan frowned and sipped his drink. "Who might that be?"

"Gail Morton. Were you here when she worked here?"

He stared at Sally and took another sip from his drink. "Yes, it was very sad when she went missing. Why now? After all this time?" His mug hit the desk, and he sprang forward in his chair. "No, don't tell me you've found her?"

"We're awaiting confirmation. A body was discovered the other day, along with a few personal items, which members of her family have recognised. The pathologist is conducting the necessary tests to verify her identity. In the meantime, we're revisiting her friends and work colleagues to see if we can gather any information that may have been missed at the time of her disappearance. Did you know her well?"

His gaze shifted to the fish tank. "Well enough. I wasn't the boss back then, so we worked out there, alongside each other on a daily basis."

"Can you recall her being unnerved about something around the time of her disappearance?"

His attention turned back to Sally. "I can't think of anything. One thing I thought was strange at the time…"

"What was that?" Sally asked.

Lorne removed her notebook and flicked it open.

"The copper in charge. He didn't appear to do much digging, if you get my drift?"

"In what respect?"

"He came to see the boss, delivered the news that she was missing and left. He didn't bother speaking to the rest of the employees, you know, her work colleagues, which I thought was a bit off."

Sally shrugged. "I run a cold case team, and for the past few years my team have had to revisit several cases with dubious outcomes."

"Bloody hell. Are we talking about police corruption here?"

Sally smiled. "I couldn't possibly comment. Moving on. What can you tell us about Gail?"

He smiled. "She was a lovely lady. Worked really well with her colleagues. She was always the one to rely on when someone was stuck about what to do with a certain case. She appeared to be the oracle to anything and everything. There wasn't a lot she didn't know about the insurance industry."

"She was missed a great deal then, when the news broke?"

"Absolutely. We were all devastated. A few of us, who worked here at the time, even set up a search party to try and find her. Going to places where we knew she used to hang out. We did that every night for two weeks or more. Nothing came of it, of course, but at least we made an effort."

Sally picked up on what she suspected was a note of bitterness. "What are you saying, that you didn't think her family made the effort to find her?"

His head tipped back, and he let out a sigh. "Make of it what you will."

"Didn't her husband have two little ones to care for back then?"

His head dropped forward, and his gaze latched on to Sally's. "And you think that's a good enough excuse not to be out there looking for your wife?"

"Don't you?" Sally challenged, her tone matching his.

"Maybe I was wrong to criticize, not being in his shoes. It's easier to say and do things when you're not having to deal with the emotional side of things, I guess."

"That's my assumption, too. What about the rest of the staff, did she get on well with everyone?"

"Yes, very well. We all thought the world..." His voice caught in his throat, and he coughed to clear it. "We all thought the world of her, and even to this day, her bright smile and laughter is severely missed around here. You ask anyone out there, we're a close-knit group, we were back then and we are now. Sometimes we talk about her, wonder what happened to her. You're not asking any questions that we haven't asked ourselves several times, during the years."

"I didn't mean to upset you."

"You haven't. I'm bitter that she's gone, that's all. Honestly, I know everyone probably tells you this about friends or loved ones who have gone missing... but she was one of the best people I've ever had the privilege of knowing."

"We're getting the picture now. Can you cast your mind back for me, try to remember if there were any clients causing her hassle around that time? Anything along those lines?"

"No. Never. She had a way of treating people that never wavered. She always put the customers' needs first. Bent over backwards to keep them as clients, whereas a lot of people would have dealt with a claim, put the phone down and given the customer a two-finger salute. She never sank to that level, ever. Actually, we often hear feedback from our customers, you know, when we send out a survey after they've renewed with us. Some of them still mention her name, and that's five years later." His voice faltered with emotion again. "I'm sorry, it still hurts, knowing that someone could go out of their way to harm her, if that's what happened."

"We can't comment on our findings at this stage. Would it be possible for us to have a quick chat with anyone who was working here at the time she went missing?"

"Everyone out there. This is a good firm to work for.

Unlike others who have a huge turnover of staff, this firm has always overcome any problems the employees might have had. I took on the role of manager this time last year and vowed to them that nothing would change between us. I respect them as much as they respect me. There aren't many bosses out there who can say that."

"You're to be admired. Do you want us to question them out there?"

"No. You can see them individually in here, if you like. I can go through my emails on one of the computers in the outer office."

"That's very kind of you. Thank you."

"Want me to send the first person in?"

"If you wouldn't mind." Sally smiled. "We shouldn't inconvenience you for too long."

He left the office.

In his absence, Lorne said, "She must have been a hell of a woman if he's still cut up about the incident."

"Exactly what I was thinking. What about the customers still mentioning her in their reviews? I've never heard the like, have you?"

"Not after five years. Maybe there is some compassion left in this world after all."

"Maybe."

The first member of staff entered the room. It was Tricia. She had tears welling up as she took her seat. "Sorry, I'm feeling a bit emotional. Alan told us what this interview is about."

"Take your time. We're not here to cause you any grief or upset, I swear."

"How can I help?"

"Simply by telling us what Gail was like to work with, that'd be a great start." Sally sipped at her now cool drink and suppressed the shudder threatening to wrack her body.

"What can I tell you, except that she was the type of person who would go to the end of the earth for you? Always put others before herself, around here anyway. I take it she was like that at home, too. Steve was a very lucky man. Not many women would carry on working full-time with two little ones to care for, I can tell you. I'm a single mother; granted, my daughter is eleven and is about to start secondary school, so things should get easier for me at home from here on out."

"How did Gail manage it?"

"Her parents did their share. They also had the funds to put the children in day care facilities as well. Damned expensive way of bringing up children if you ask me."

"Each to their own. Did you ever see her have an argument with another member of staff?"

"Never. Not in a million years. She was always the one keeping the peace if anyone fell out, which wasn't very often."

"Can you remember back to around the time she went missing? Did she confide in you, possibly mention that she had something on her mind that was troubling her?"

Tricia's eyes narrowed as she thought. "No, nothing is coming to mind. She always had a smile on her face. Even if she was troubled, it was hard to tell. I suppose we always have grief to deal with at home now and again, but she wasn't the type to bring it to work."

"In other words, she was the ultimate professional."

Tricia pointed and nodded. "That's it. Spot on."

"Okay. Then that concludes our interview. See, it wasn't that bad, was it?"

"No. Thank you. Shall I send the next one in?"

"If you would. Thank you for speaking with us."

She smiled, pushed her chair back and left the room.

"I can't see us getting any further here, can you?" Sally asked.

"Nope."

Sally's phone rang. She answered it. "Hello. Sally Parker. How can I help?"

"Boss, it's Jordan. We've received an anxious call, and I thought you should be aware of it right away."

"Anxious? About what?"

"The neighbour of Steve Morton has just contacted us. She was looking after the children and told me that she peered out of the window because Steve was due home and saw him being bundled into a red Qashqai."

"Shit. Who by?"

"A heavily built man wearing jogging pants and a T-shirt. The neighbour took down the registration number. I've run it through the system, and the car is registered to Phil Thomas."

"Fuck. Okay, we'll get over there. Put out the usual alerts at your end. I'll ring his parents on the way, see what they have to say about this."

"Alerts actioned, boss. I'll keep in touch should anything else come up."

"Thanks, Jordan." Sally jabbed the End Call button and shot out of her seat. "Sod this, we need to get moving, *now*."

"I totally agree. It's not like we're getting very far here."

In the doorway, they bumped into a man with a shaved head and numerous piercings.

"Sorry, I was told you wanted to see me."

"It's going to have to wait. We'll be back another time, there's been a major development in the case."

Sally and Lorne pushed past him, and Sally threw another apology over her shoulder before they hit the pavement outside.

"A quick question, if I may be so bold," Lorne said.

Sally paused mid-stride. "Go on, you don't need to seek my permission. Spit it out."

"Do we know Phil's address? We met him at his parents' house. Did they mention if he lived with them?"

"Damn, you're right. Why didn't I think about that? Don't answer, it was a rhetorical question. Ring Jordan back and get the address while I phone the parents."

"That's another thing... umm... not wishing to step on the tips of your size fives, I wouldn't ring ahead, I would use the element of surprise on them."

"I knew there was a reason I chose you to be my partner over the others. Make the call. I'll use the siren to get us across town quickly."

"After I've made the call, right? Otherwise, I won't be able to hear Jordan's reply."

"How do you do that?"

Halfway across the road towards the car, Lorne asked, "Do what?"

"Have a bloody good response to every obstacle put in your way."

"Ah, that's easy. It's called years of experience living with my ex, Tom Simpkins."

They both laughed, and Sally opened the car with her key fob.

Lorne rang the station as soon as she'd belted herself in and put the phone on speaker. "Jordan, it's me. Something we forgot to ask during the last call."

"What's that, Lorne?"

"We haven't got Phil's address."

"Ah, yes, it's my fault, I was going to check but I forgot. It's fifty-seven Keswick Road, not far from where his parents live."

"Got it. We're en route now. Be in touch soon."

"Good luck. I'm going to call in a few favours, see if I can get the CCTV footage from around that area. I've already requested the information for the ANPRs."

"Excellent work." Lorne ended the call and grinned. "That young man is going to be seeking promotion sooner than you anticipated, you mark my words."

"I saw something in him when he came for the interview. Reminded me of a younger version of Jack, when he had all the enthusiasm of youth on his side. That's somewhat dwindled in recent years, about the time the DCI approached me about setting up the team."

"He seems to have got over his threat to chuck in the towel these days, or am I missing something?"

"Yeah, he seems a bit more settled these days. Who knows if losing his dad this week will alter things again? Oh, I forgot to mention, he's coming back in a couple of days."

Lorne rubbed her hands together as if she were trying to start a fire with two sticks whilst stuck out in the middle of the wilderness. "We'd better make sure we solve the case by the time he gets back then."

Sally laughed. "I had a feeling you were going to say something similar."

"Glad I didn't disappoint you then. You know me, I'm never one to walk away from an intriguing investigation and, I have to say, this one has me hooked."

"Me, too. I wish it could be straightforward, though. Umm... just a thought, would it be worth ringing Carol, see if she can give us any indication where Phil has taken Steve?"

"Let's put that on hold for now, until we're desperate. It's not something she often comes up with, if you get what I mean?"

"Okay, we'll do it the old-fashioned way, for now."

## CHAPTER 9

They called at Phil's home. There was no sign of his vehicle, and when they knocked on the door there was no one home. Sally and Lorne even checked with the neighbours on either side. Neither of them had seen hide nor hair of him since the previous day. Defeated, they drove the short distance to the parents' house. They drew up outside. The couple's car was parked in the road at the front.

"Looks like we're in luck," Lorne said.

"It does. Let's hope they're not the type to defend their son, no matter what he gets up to."

"I think you're living in a dream world if you believe that... just saying."

"Only one way to find out."

They left the car and walked up the path to the front door. Sally rang the bell.

It took Jan a while to answer. She wiped her hands on a tea towel and stared at them. "Oh, hello. I was in the kitchen, washing up. Do you need to come in and speak with us?"

"If it's not an intrusion, thanks, Jan." Sally had every intention of remaining calm, hoping the husband-and-wife team would drop some kind of hint as to where their son had taken Steve.

"Not at all. Andrew is in the greenhouse, I'll give him a shout. Once the tomatoes start bearing fruit it's like an obsession with him. Loves nothing more than to sit there, staring at the plants, watching them ripen. Of course they don't, but there's no telling him." She smiled and retreated backwards, allowing them to enter.

Neither Sally nor Lorne smiled in return.

"Oh dear, has something happened?" Jan was quick to ask.

"If you can ask your husband to join us, we'll tell you both at the same time."

She left them and tore through the house. "Andrew, Andrew, where the hell are you? Get in here, right now. The police are here."

The couple joined Sally and Lorne in the hallway.

"What's going on? Do you have news for us?" Andrew demanded.

"Why don't we make ourselves comfortable?" Sally suggested.

"Sorry, yes, come through to the lounge," Jan said. She opened the door and was the first to enter the room. She remained standing, wiping her hands nervously on the tea towel.

Sally and Lorne took their seats on the sofa, and Sally gestured for the couple to do the same.

It wasn't until they were seated that Sally cleared her throat and said, "I have to ask if you've heard from Phil today."

The couple frowned and glanced at each other.

"I haven't, have you, Andrew?"

Jan's husband shook his head and then asked, "What's going on? Has he done something wrong?"

"You could say that. We have reason to believe that Phil

has abducted Steve. What we're hoping you can tell us is where he might be heading."

"What? Oh no, why would he?" Jan asked, clearly shaken by the news.

"Because he's a bloody numbskull, that's why," Andrew replied. "I told him not to do anything rash. As usual, he didn't take a blind bit of notice. Never does. Always bloody listens to his mother, though, it's always been the same."

"Don't start, Andrew, the officers don't want to know about the spats we've had over the years. This is serious."

"Don't you think I know that, woman?" Andrew raised a hand and let it drop onto the arm of the chair, clearly frustrated.

Sally sighed. "Please, you two falling out isn't going to help us. What we need to know is if Phil has been in touch with you today."

"No, not at all," Jan said. "Let me get my phone, I've been doing some baking all morning. I needed a distraction to stop my mind working overtime after dealing with the news you delivered the last time you were here." She left the room and returned to show Sally the phone. "Nothing, no messages or phone calls, as you can see. What in God's name is he up to?"

"Can you call him? See if he'll pick up? It would be better if he gave himself up now. If he doesn't, I'll have no other option than to get a team of officers out there to hunt him down. This is serious. I saw how angry he was during our conversation the other day. There's no telling what he's going to do to Steve. We need to stop it now, before things get out of hand."

"Of course we do. I swear, we have no knowledge about his intentions, do we, Andrew?"

"None whatsoever. We would never allow him to harm Steve, never," Andrew confirmed.

"Please, you must try and help us. Can you think of anywhere he might have taken Steve?"

The couple stared at each other and shook their heads.

"No, I can't think of anywhere," Jan replied. She buried her head in her hands and sobbed.

Andrew comforted her, if a little reluctantly at first. "Come on now, Jan. What's the use in breaking down like this, it's not going to get us very far, is it?"

She dropped her hands and glared at her husband. "Men, you have no bloody idea. Women need to let it out, it's our release valve. I'm sure the officers would agree with me, wouldn't you, ladies?"

"Sometimes, yes. Please, try and remain calm. What about another property he has keys to and uses? We stopped off at his house before we came here, but there was no sign of him."

"I can't think of anywhere, can you, love?" Jan asked. She gripped her husband's hand in both of hers.

"No. Not at all. We're not being much help, are we?" Andrew replied.

"It's fine, either you know or you don't. If he left the area, where would he be likely to go? Does he have a favourite place he likes to visit?"

"Cromer area, but he hasn't been up there for a while," Andrew told them.

"Yes, that would make sense. Why has he done this, why?" Jan broke down again.

"We don't know, but believe me, we won't stop until we've found your son. Please, can you at least try to call him?"

Jan picked up her mobile and rang Phil's number, but it rang five times and then went into voicemail. "Phil, where are you? What have you done? If you hurt Steve, I will never forgive you. You can't take the law into your own hands like this, you just can't. Come home. Inspector Parker has told me that if you give yourself up now, it'll be better for everyone. Come home, son, come home. Or ring me, let's discuss this over the phone, if that's what you'd prefer to do. Get in touch with us, before it's too late. The police are blocking all the roads, they have gathered men from another force, it's serious what you've done. Come home, Phil, for God's sake, think of Haydon and Rory. Don't be rash and do anything to harm... shit, the message ran out, it was too long."

"It doesn't matter, you emphasised the point well. Thank you," Sally said. She rose to her feet and gave Jan her business card. "Please ring me if he gets in touch with you. Would you pick the kids up from school?"

"Gosh yes, of course I will. You have to believe us, we're devastated Phil has done this, just devastated."

"I agree. When I get my hands on him..." Andrew added.

Sally smiled. "I'll pretend I didn't hear that, Mr Thomas."

The couple walked them back to the front door.

"Keep trying Phil's number, if you will?" Sally asked.

"Of course. You can count on us," Andrew said.

On the way to the car, Lorne peered over her shoulder and asked, "Do you believe them?"

"I think so. I take it you have doubts."

"Something about them doesn't ring true, but ignore me if you're not receiving the same signals I am."

"For now, I will." Sally opened the car door and slipped on her seatbelt. She pulled away from the kerb and then drew up ahead of a few nearby parked cars.

"What are you doing?"

"I want to wait here for a moment or two, see if either of them leaves the house. If they do, we'll follow them."

"Ah, so your gut is telling you something after all."

Sally winked at Lorne. "You're not the only one who has ever relied on their gut instinct over the years, Lorne Warner."

"Consider me told." Lorne giggled. She twisted in her seat to observe the house. "Nothing yet. Want to have a bet? I reckon five minutes."

"Nope. I think it'll be less than that."

The front door of the house opened, and Mr Thomas walked up the path and in the opposite direction.

"Interesting," Sally said. "Why set off on foot? I wonder if they've cottoned on that we're here and are trying to fool us. We'll sit tight, see if she appears and jumps in the car."

"In the meantime, he's getting away," Lorne voiced her concern.

"Give it time. Two minutes. If she doesn't leave the house then we'll go after him."

The two minutes dragged by. Eventually, Sally heaved out an impatient sigh and proceeded to make a three-point turn in the road. When they drove past the house, Jan stood at the window, looking in the direction her husband had set off in.

"I'm wondering if things got a little heated and he stormed out," Lorne was the first to suggest.

"Possibly. She seemed a bit anxious back there."

They soon caught up with Andrew. He was walking briskly.

Lorne pointed ahead. "Want to take another bet?"

Sally glanced in the direction of her pointed finger. "The pub. He's off to drown his sorrows."

"Yep. Why do men have to do that? Take off rather than deal with the important issue in hand? I bet his wife needed consoling after we left, and here he is…"

"Yeah, let's not try to fathom men out, we'd be here all year and never find an answer. Let's get back to the station, see what's going on there."

Lorne tapped her watch. "We've got an appointment in half an hour, aren't you going to keep it?"

Sally slammed a fist onto the steering wheel, pulled over

and turned the car around. "It had slipped my mind for a moment."

THE LAST CUSTOMER left the café and, from where they were parked, they could see the staff clearing the tables and flitting around the inside, eager to get away. At three-fifty, the staff left via the side entrance. Sally and Lorne exited the car and walked across the road.

Linda Shaw smiled, recognising them. "Ah, here they are now. This is my sister, Lorraine."

"Nice to meet you, Lorraine," Sally said. "I take it Linda has explained the situation to you?"

"She has. We're both still in shock. How can we help with your investigation?"

"Can we speak in our car?" Sally asked.

"Yes, I don't mind, do you, Lorraine?"

"Not at all."

The four of them returned to the vehicle, and Sally and Lorne twisted in their seats to speak to the two sisters.

"We really appreciate you talking to us," Sally said. "We know how upsetting the situation must be for you right now."

"It's okay. I suppose all our grieving was done when Gail first went missing," Linda replied.

"I agree. I guess we've been waiting to hear this type of news for years. To tell you the truth, we feel a bit numb, don't we, Linda?"

"Yes, that's how I feel, numb. What is it you want to know?"

"It's hard to come to terms with your emotions when something like this occurs. We won't keep you long, I promise. What we're trying to ascertain is if anything was going on in Gail's life at the time of her disappearance. As her best friends, I thought you might be able to help us."

The two sisters snuck a glance at each other but remained quiet, raising Sally's suspicions.

"Please, if there is anything you can tell us, it might lead us to the killer. Don't you want to see the person punished?"

"Absolutely." Linda sighed. "I have to tell her, it's important they should know, Lorraine."

Her sister shrugged. "On your head be it."

"What? Don't say that. They need to hear the truth," Linda countered, her voice rising a few pitches.

"Which is what?" Sally jumped in before Linda had time to reconsider her decision.

"She was having an affair," Linda mumbled.

Sally shot Lorne a look and fidgeted in her seat. "What? And this was kept a secret from the investigating officer at the time of her disappearance? Why?"

"Because we didn't want to add to the family's distress," Lorraine added. She clutched her sister's hand. "We've lived with this secret all these years, been tempted numerous times to let the cat out of the bag, but we wouldn't have been able to live with the consequences. Steve was ripped apart as it was. He had the two kids to care for, we didn't want to add to his misery or to turn him against Gail when she wasn't around to defend herself. It wasn't our responsibility to mention the affair."

"Maybe not to the family, but there's no way you should have kept quiet about it to the officer in charge. Bloody hell." Sally tucked a stray hair behind her ear. "Who was Gail having an affair with?"

It was Lorraine who answered, "Someone at work."

"Shit, we were there earlier, questioning the staff, but we got called away because something important cropped up. Who? Come on, ladies, you have to tell us. I know if I were in your shoes, I'd want to know the truth about my best friend's death." Sally pulled out the guilt card, hoping it would force the sisters' hands.

"We have to tell them, Lorraine, I can't live with this any longer."

Her sister shrugged. "You tell them, I want nothing to do with it."

"Why, Lorraine? Why sit on the truth, especially now we believe Gail's body has been found and we know her killer is still out there?" Sally urged, her heart racing.

Linda gasped. "That's right, we have to reveal the truth. What if the killer comes after us?"

"Jesus, and you think telling the truth is going to prevent that from happening, Linda? Grow up. The killer knows the truth, they're probably aware that we know it, too."

"Not necessarily, Lorraine," Sally butted in. "If that were the case, don't you think the killer would have come after you by now?"

Lorraine tipped her head back against the headrest. "I can't deal with this."

Linda shook her sister by the shoulders and shouted, "Stop thinking about yourself all the damn time. This is important. If you cared one iota about Gail, you'll tell the officers. Sod it, if you don't tell them, I will."

"You do it then."

Linda shifted in her seat to face Sally and Lorne. "It was Alan Victor. They'd been having an affair for a couple of months."

"Wow, okay. We spoke to him earlier, and he never mentioned it. Did anyone else know?" Sally replied.

"No, she swore us to secrecy."

"Was it a fling, or were they serious about each other?" Sally probed.

"I think things were getting that way. It was difficult,

what with her being married and having the two children," Linda confirmed.

"What about Alan, was he married at the time?"

"No. But I think he had a girlfriend."

"Interesting." Sally nodded. "Did she mention if he was ever violent towards her?"

Linda adamantly shook her head. "Goodness, no, that's inconceivable. She would never have put up with that crap, and if Phil had ever found out, he would have crucified Alan."

"Her brother Phil? Were they really close?"

"Exceptionally close. He protected her. All throughout our schooldays, he was there, watching out for her in case anyone caused her trouble. There were only two years between them. Even when he left school, he used to be there to meet her at the gates some days, rather than let her walk home alone."

"That explains what's happened," Sally said to Lorne.

"What's going on?" Linda demanded. "He's always been a bit of a thug. Hit first before he engaged his brain. What's he done?"

Sally chewed on her lip and then revealed the truth. "He's abducted Steve, Gail's husband."

"Oh fuck. Shit, he's always had a sneaky suspicion that Steve was behind her disappearance. You've got to find him, he's likely to kill Steve."

"We're doing our very best. How well do you know Phil?"

"Not very well," Linda replied.

Sally noticed the colour had risen in Lorraine's cheeks. "Lorraine? What about you?"

"I sort of had a crush on him when we were teenagers."

"And are you still friendly now?"

She rolled her eyes. "If you're asking if I still have his phone number then no, I don't."

"That's a shame. This is a long shot, but I have to ask.

When you were growing up and all hanging around together, if you did, was there anywhere in particular you liked to hang out in this area?"

"When Phil was given his first car by his parents, he took us on a few rides to Thetford."

"Any place in particular?"

"Not that I can remember. There are a few areas down there where boy racers used to hang out. This was years ago. I'm betting your lot have put a stop to that sort of carry-on these days," Linda replied.

"What about hideouts, an old barn or something along those lines?" Sally asked.

The sisters shook their heads.

"Sorry, can't think of anything," Lorraine spoke for the pair of them.

"It doesn't matter. We're going to have to make a move now. If I give you my card and you think of anything you feel we should consider for the investigation, will you give me a call?"

Sally handed each of them a card, and they popped them into their pockets.

"We'll try and think back to around the time Gail went missing. If we remember anything, you'll be the first to know," Linda said.

"That's all we can ask. We appreciate you speaking with us. Take care, ladies."

The sisters said goodbye and left the car.

"We need to get back to the station," Sally said.

"What about Victor?" Lorne strapped herself in and asked.

"I don't think he's going anywhere soon, at least I hope not. I want to do some extra digging on him before we go round there and pull him in for questioning."

# CHAPTER 10

They arrived back at the station to find Joanna on a call. She glanced their way with a wide-eyed expression that made Sally's stomach clench into a tight knot.

"Looks ominous. Get us a coffee, if you will, Lorne?"

"On my way."

Sally approached Joanna's desk. "What's going on?" she asked once Joanna hung up.

"Interesting call from an anonymous young lady, who told me she's been sitting on some information for days, wondering what to do about it."

"For days? So this has nothing to do with Phil abducting Steve then? I had hoped it was about that."

"No, this is to do with the press conference you put out last week."

"Fuck. Why has it taken so long for her to get in touch? Not that it matters. What did she have to say?"

"She told me it was about the body found in the lake."

"I gathered that much, Joanna. What about it? Can she confirm the identity of the remains?"

"Yes. Confirmed, and she's given me a possible suspect's name."

"What?" Sally took the offered mug from Lorne and perched on the nearby desk. "Who?"

"James Trout. He's her boyfriend, apparently. They got into a fight, and he let slip that she would be next. Once he'd calmed down, she asked him what he meant, and he admitted that five years ago he killed a woman. She was horrified at the time but tried to play it cool so she could get more information out of him. He mentioned it was some kind of game that went wrong... and that they dumped the body in the lake. She put two and two together and has been going out of her mind with worry ever since."

"A game gone wrong, that's what Carol mentioned. She was right," Lorne stated then took a sip from her mug.

"I know you don't want to get her involved but I think you should let her know. She might be able to tell us where Phil is. Wait a minute... you said *they* dumped the body, so there were at least two of them."

Joanna nodded. "So it would seem. I asked her if she had further information but I could hear the fear resonating in her voice. She ended the call after that."

"Don't worry. Can you see what you can find out about James Trout for me? I need to have a think about where we go from here."

"I'll get on it now."

"Stuart, I need you to do some digging on Alan Victor, the new owner of Robinson's Insurance. Just to bring you all up to date, we've been informed by Gail's best friends that she was having an affair with Victor. Somehow, during our interview with him earlier on today, he avoided telling us that vital information. I want to know why. Is he hiding something?" Sally instructed.

"Want me to check the social media platforms, see if

Victor and Trout know each other?" Lorne asked. "You're thinking they might be friends, involved in this game?"

Sally took a sip from her coffee and shrugged. "I'm thinking Trout was with either Phil or Alan at the time of her death. Saying that, I can't see her brother being involved, can you?"

Lorne adamantly shook her head.

"What would you do, Lorne?"

"If all this landed on my desk, I would leave the patrols to track down Phil and concentrate the team's efforts on working with the information we have to hand. Which is what you're doing. Maybe strike while the iron is hot and bring them both in for questioning, Trout and Victor."

Sally placed her finger and thumb on either side of her chin. "You're right. First, we need to spend the next half an hour carrying out the necessary background checks. Let's see if we can find any links between either James Trout and Alan Victor or Phil Thomas."

The team put their heads down, and it wasn't long before Sally had Victor's and Trout's addresses to hand. "What about any connections via social media, Lorne?"

"Nothing found, sorry."

"Not to worry. Jordan, I want you and Stuart to go to Trout's address. If he's there, bring him in for questioning. Lorne, you and I will go over to the insurance office…" Sally glanced at the clock on the wall. "It's almost six. No, we shouldn't waste time, we'll go directly to his home, have a chat with him there. If we don't like what he has to say then we'll haul his arse in."

"Sounds good to me," Lorne said.

"Let's go."

. . .

ARMED WITH VICTOR'S home address, Sally and Lorne headed over there, while Jordan and Stuart went in the opposite direction to pick Trout up. Sally had instructed Jordan to contact her, once the suspect had been located. Meanwhile, Joanna was left holding the fort, monitoring the CCTV and ANPRs in the area, on the lookout for Phil, whom Sally presumed was in hiding by now.

"This is a posh area," Lorne was the first to comment as they drew into the fairly new executive estate with only six houses on the site.

"I remember when these were built a few years ago, the asking price was over a million."

"I'm not surprised. Look at the size of the plot they're all sitting on. Not that I'm envious or anything."

They both laughed.

"Yeah, right."

There were two Audis sitting on Victor's drive, one newer than the other. The front garden was neatly bordered by a knee-high boxed hedge. Sally rang the bell. The door was answered a few seconds later by a slim redhead in her mid-to-late thirties.

She appraised each of them and then asked, "Yes. Who are you?"

Sally and Lorne flashed their IDs. The woman gasped and seemed taken aback.

"We're here to see Alan Victor, are you his wife?" Sally asked.

"No, I'm his partner. We're due to get married in the next few years, time permitting. What's this about?"

"Is he in?" Sally asked, ignoring the woman's question.

"Yes. I suppose you'd better come in."

Sally and Lorne wiped their feet on the mat outside and then entered the spacious hallway.

"Come through to the lounge."

Sally gave a brief nod. "Have you been together long?"

"Around six years, why?"

"Just making polite conversation," Sally retorted.

The woman opened the lounge door and said, "Alan, there are two police officers here to see you, but they're refusing to tell me what it's about. Care to enlighten me?"

Alan was sitting at a small desk in the corner, using his laptop. "Something and nothing, we spoke earlier. Can you get the ladies a drink, Dee?"

"Do I have to? I've got the dinner to prepare yet."

Sally raised a hand. "Don't bother on our account, we've not long had one. If you wouldn't mind leaving us alone for a few minutes, this won't take long."

Dee bustled back to the door, complaining as she went, "It had better not. You've spoilt my evening already by showing up on our doorstep. I dread to think what the neighbours are likely to say about this."

"It's a good job we didn't turn up in a patrol car then, isn't it?" Sally couldn't resist firing at her before she slammed the door shut.

"Sorry about that, she's a moody cow at the best of times. Her nose has been put out of joint because you wouldn't tell her what's going on."

"So I gathered," Sally replied. "Shall we take a seat?"

"Sorry, yes, please do. Did you forget to ask me something earlier?"

"No. But it has since come to our attention that you might have possibly forgotten to tell us something important that could shed a different light on our investigation."

"Such as?" He frowned and sat on the sofa nearest to the window.

Sally and Lorne sat on the other leather sofa a few feet away from him.

"Such as… you were having an affair with Gail Morton at

the time she went missing. May I ask why you chose to keep that fact from us?"

"I... umm... I didn't think it was important."

"Not *important*? You must be joking. Why keep such a vital piece of information from us? It can only mean you have something to hide. Do you?"

"How dare you? No, I have nothing to hide."

The door opened, and Dee came back in. "Don't mind me, I'm only after my phone to look up a recipe I found on the internet the other day. Everything all right in here? Alan, why do you look so guilty?"

"It's nothing. You're imagining things as usual. You were asked to leave us alone. Now do it, Dee."

She chuntered something indecipherable under her breath, stomped out and again slammed the door shut behind her.

"It would appear that Dee gets upset easily when she believes she's being kept in the dark about something," Sally suggested.

"Don't most women?"

"I don't think so. Going back to your affair, weren't you going out with Dee at the time?"

"How do you know that?"

Sally tapped the side of her nose. "Maybe it's because I'm a shit-hot detective."

He shrugged. "What about it?"

"Did she know about the affair?"

He peered over his shoulder at the door, and sweat broke out on his forehead. "Did she heck. Do you think she'd still be around if she did? Does she seem the type to forgive and forget?"

"So why take the chance? Why have the affair in the first place if you knew it would mean the end of your relationship with Dee?"

He stared at the floor close to Sally's feet and mumbled, "I was younger then and... well, Gail was like a magnet. Every man she came into contact with was drawn to her, including me."

"How far did the affair go? Were you serious about each other? How long had it been going on?"

"I was serious, but Gail had grave doubts and wanted to end it. She wasn't getting the attention she deserved at home, from Steve, you know what I mean, in the bedroom. I was happy to oblige. The affair lasted a couple of months, right up until she went missing."

"Did you have anything to do with that?" Sally pushed, her eyes narrowing, doing her best to unnerve him. She was struggling to make him out, couldn't tell if he was speaking the truth or not.

He surprised her by launching himself out of the chair. "No, I could never harm her. Never. I *loved* her."

"Sit down, Mr Victor," Sally warned.

He flopped back into his chair, his shoulders slumped in defeat. "You have to believe me. We were out there a number of days for her. I need to know the truth for my own sanity."

"I'm going to throw a name your way. I'm expecting a truthful answer from you."

"I promise."

"James Trout. Do you recognise that name?"

He thought for a moment and then shook his head. "Can't say I do. Should I?"

"It's a lead we're considering at the moment. To be honest with you, Alan, because we've had to come out to see you this evening, having spoken to you earlier and you neglecting to tell us the truth about your affair, I'm not entirely sure I can trust anything you've told us this evening. Therefore, I think it would be better if you accompanied us to the station for questioning."

"What? No way. I swear, I've been truthful. I have nothing to do with Gail going missing and I haven't got the foggiest idea who this frigging man is. You have to believe me, please, I'm begging you." He slapped his hands together as if in prayer.

Sally cast a sideways glance at Lorne just as Sally's phone rang. "I need to get this. Hi, Jordan. What have you got for me?"

"We've got Trout, boss. We're on our way back to the station."

"That's great news. Did he put up a fight?"

"No. It was as though he was expecting us to come knocking for him."

"Interesting. Is he there?"

"He's in the car with Stuart."

"Has he told you anything yet?"

"No, he just held out his hands, and we slapped the cuffs on."

"Okay, we're just about finished here. We'll see you back at the station." Sally ended the call. "How well do you know Phil Thomas?" Sally asked.

His brow furrowed. "Not very well. I think I met him a couple of times when a group of us ended up at the pub after work. Why do you ask?"

"It's my prerogative," she replied swiftly. "I'm going to need you to come with us. If you refuse to, it'll only make matters worse."

"Why? I don't understand why. What have I done except have an affair with Gail? I'm innocent, you can't pin anything on me."

"Maybe not, but the fact that you withheld the truth about your affair earlier has put severe doubts in my mind that I'm struggling to shift."

"Jesus, you're so wrong about this. Who is this man you were asking me about?"

"Another piece of the puzzle we're unsure about. Get your shoes and your jacket, you're accompanying us to the station."

"What? Can't I take my own car?"

"No, we'll arrange a lift home for you, once we've interviewed you under caution."

His head jutted forward. "Under caution? You can't do this. I'm innocent, I haven't done anything wrong, you have to believe me."

"Apart from avoiding to tell us vital information about your affair with a dead person." Sally stood, and Lorne followed suit. "Do we need to use our cuffs or are you going to come willingly?"

"No. I'll come quietly. You're making a dreadful mistake about this."

"We'll see. You'd better tell Dee you'll be a couple of hours."

"What reason shall I give for you dragging me down to the station?"

"You're helping us with our enquiries."

He sighed and ran a trembling hand over his face. "Okay."

The three of them entered the hallway.

Dee was lingering by the kitchen doorway. "Are you off now?"

"Yes, they're going. I won't be long, love."

Dee seemed confused. "Sorry, what are you talking about?"

"I'm going with them. I'll be back soon. I'm helping them with their enquiries."

"In relation to what? What are you keeping from me, Alan?"

Sally decided to jump in. "We have a few questions

relating to a former colleague of Mr Victor's. He shouldn't be more than a couple of hours."

"This is ridiculous. Why can't you hold the interview here?" Dee ranted.

"It's for the best," Sally replied. "We'll give Mr Victor a lift back later. There's really no need for you to be concerned."

"Like fuck. That's easy for you to say. What about his dinner? It's nearly ready! What am I supposed to do with that?"

"Do you have a microwave?" Sally grinned.

"Screw you, lady."

"Thank you. We'll be off now."

Sally, Lorne and Alan Victor left the house, and Lorne closed the door behind them. Something thudded against it as they made their way up the path to the car.

"I think Dee needs to take a chill pill," Sally stated.

"She's always been a little hot-headed. A typical redhead. She'll be fine in a few hours," he said.

Lorne placed Alan in the back of the car and jumped in beside Sally.

BACK AT THE STATION, they put Alan in Interview Room One while they had a quick conversation with Jordan and Stuart. "We're going to swap over. I'm going to ask you and Stuart to interview Alan Victor while Lorne and I tackle James Trout. Has Trout said anything further on the way in?"

"No, tight-lipped all the way, boss. How do you want to play it with Victor?"

"He didn't actually lie to us earlier, he avoided telling us the truth about his affair. Try and work on him. I'm not sure whether I've done the right thing or not by bringing him in, but who knows? Being in an interview room might break down some barriers. Let me know how you're getting on, if anything interesting comes up during the interview."

"Will do, boss. Good luck with Trout."

"Thanks." Sally had already arranged for the desk sergeant to supply them with drinks after a few minutes. "Let's get this over with. Are you ready?" Sally asked Lorne.

"I'm up for it. Got my second wind back in the car. It has been a long day."

Sally sucked in a huge breath and let it out. "I have a feeling we're closing in fast, hence me wanting to stick with it and not leave things overnight."

"I'm inclined to agree with you. There's also Steve's life at risk, something we need to remember."

"I haven't forgotten, partner."

They entered the room to find a man in his mid-thirties, with long brown hair, sitting hunched over the melamine desk and a male constable standing at the back wall. Sally smiled at the PC and then took her seat at the desk with Lorne right beside her.

Lorne said the usual spiel for the recording before Sally began the interview in earnest.

"Mr Trout, or can I call you, James?"

He looked up and flicked his hair over his shoulders. "James will do. Why am I here?"

"We have reason to believe that you were involved in a malicious crime five years ago. Can you confirm this?"

"No comment."

*Shit, might have known that was coming. Don't give up, Sal.*

"Have you seen the local news lately?"

"Yeah, what about it?"

"You might have seen me putting out a request for any information relating to a body that was found in Cavendish Lake."

"And?"

"Someone contacted us earlier today, informing us that you know what happened to the victim."

After shuffling in his seat, he flung himself back. "I do. It's been playing on my mind. I can't sleep, eat, or even think straight right now."

"Carry on. The more you're willing to divulge at this stage, the more lenient a judge is bound to be when the case gets to court."

Trout paused, his head dipped to his chest, and then he stared at the ceiling. "It was *her* fault."

"Sorry, who are you talking about?"

"She had me over a barrel. I got involved in this stupid truth or dare game. She would carry out a task for me, if I would do the same for her."

"Who?" Sally urged. When he refused to answer, she tried a different tack. "All right, what did she have to do for her side of the bargain?"

"I was having a problem with my boss at the time… she killed her for me."

"What? What was the name of the victim? Has the body ever been discovered?"

"No. Her name was… Tania Benjamin. We followed her on a night out with her friends and did the deed."

"You put her in the river at Great Yarmouth, didn't you?"

He nodded his confirmation.

"And in return, you killed Gail Morton, is that correct?"

"Yes. I got caught up in the thrill of it all. It wasn't until that bitch expected me to cut up the body that it dawned on me what we'd done."

"Who was the other person, James?"

Covering his eyes with his hands, he let out a long sigh. "I can't tell you that. She knows where I live. We've kept in touch over the years, and she drops hints now and again that she'll come after my family and friends if ever I tell anyone."

"Via text message or via social media?"

"Facebook. Shit, I shouldn't have told you that, should I? I'm such a dick at times if I'm worried about something."

"You said it yourself. There's no going back from this, James, not now you've admitted your involvement in two murders, therefore, what have you got to lose by telling us? If she gets wind of you being pulled in for questioning, won't that cause alarm bells to ring in her head?" Sally asked, upping the ante in the hope he would reconsider his decision.

The way his gaze flitted around the room it was obvious that he was wavering. Finally, after he expelled another large breath, he mumbled, "Dee."

Lorne nudged Sally's knee under the table, and Sally's blood flowed rapidly through her veins.

"Sorry, I didn't quite catch that. Can you repeat the name, James?"

"Dee, Dee Armstrong."

Sally shook her head. Was she hearing things? Dee wasn't a very common name, and yet they had met a feisty woman going by that name earlier, at Victor's house. She stood and tipped her chair back. "DS Warner, can you bring the interview to a close, there's someone I need to speak to."

Sally charged out of the room and entered the interview room next door. Jordan glanced up and announced her arrival for the recording. "I have one question I need to direct to Mr Victor."

Alan twisted in his chair to face her. "What's that?"

"What is Dee's surname?"

"Armstrong. Why? What does she have to do with this?"

"Plenty, by the sounds of it. Wrap this interview up, guys. We'll all be setting off soon."

"What about my lift back home?" Alan was quick to ask.

"Don't worry, we'll be heading your way and can drop

you off." Sally winked at Jordan and then Stuart. "I'll see you outside in a few minutes."

Sally left the room and paced the hallway until Lorne, Jordan and Stuart appeared. "It's her. His girlfriend is the killer. We have James Trout's confession. We should all go to Victor's address and pick her up. We can make out we're innocently dropping him off, as agreed, and then pounce. I think we can safely assume that she'll put up a fight, judging by the mood she was in when we met her at the house earlier. I'll get the desk sergeant to deal with Trout, get him charged and safely tucked away in a cell. Hopefully, his accomplice will be joining him within the hour."

## CHAPTER 11

Sally drove, her stomach churning constantly during the trip back to the executive estate. She couldn't help wondering if the neighbours' curtains would be twitching once everything kicked off.

"Are you all right?" Lorne asked.

"Yes, why do you ask?"

"I'm kind of feeling sorry for the steering wheel right now. Your knuckles are so white, it looks like you're throttling it."

"Oops." Sally shrugged and released her grip. "How are you doing?"

"Fine, relaxed. Also ready to nail her fucking arse to the wall if she tries to kick off." Lorne grinned and blinked rapidly.

"You're frigging nuts. I bet you are. It's been a while since you've had a scrap in the line of duty, eh?"

"You could say that. I think I'm due one. Bring it on, I say."

They both laughed. Lorne had a way of making her feel at ease. The estate came into view ahead of them, and Sally slowed down. They exited the vehicle and made their way over to Jordan's car to retrieve Alan Victor.

"I still don't understand why it takes four of you to bring me home. Are you going to fill me in?"

"I told you, we're en route to another job. Come on, we'll show you to the door."

"No disrespect, Inspector, but I think I can make it to my own front door. I'm not likely to get lost when I'm within a few feet of it, now am I?"

"Humour me," Sally replied with a smile.

Alan tutted, and the four detectives walked with him up the path.

He opened the door with his key and turned to face them. "Thank you. That's me safely home now."

"Glad to hear it. Can you call Dee, please?"

His frown deepened. "Why?"

"We'd like to personally hand you back over to her, safe and sound."

"Dee, I'm home. Where are you?" Alan shouted.

"I'm in the bedroom."

"She's upstairs. She likes to have a soak in the bath around this time of night."

"Ask her to come down and see you," Sally said, her smile still firmly in place but her insides squeezing tighter with each passing second.

"Can you come down, hon? I have a surprise for you."

"No, you come up here. I'm reading. You're the one who went off. I've done my work for the day. You can sod off if you think I'm coming down there to get your dinner ready for you. It's in the oven, dried up, no doubt, by now. This is *me* time."

Sally had heard enough. She gestured for the others to join her and tore up the stairs, two at a time.

"Hey, you can't come in here uninvited," Alan yelled behind them.

*Want to bet? We have a killer who needs taking into custody. She's roamed free, unchallenged all these years. I dread to think what else she's been guilty of in that time. Hey, man, take it from me, you're bloody lucky to be alive.*

Sally barged into the bedroom with Lorne, Jordan and Stuart on her heels, to find a stunned-looking Dee, reading her Kindle on top of the quilt.

Throwing her device aside, she dropped her legs to the floor and demanded, "What's the meaning of this intrusion?"

"Dee Armstrong, I'm arresting you for the murder of Tania Benjamin and Gail Morton. You do not have to say anything. But, it may harm your defence if you do not mention when questioned something which you later rely on in court. Anything you do say may be given in evidence."

"What? I don't know what you're talking about. I don't know either of the women concerned." She glanced behind Sally. "Alan, tell them they've made a mistake."

"What have you done, Dee? The police never make mistakes of this magnitude."

Dee stamped her foot and sneered at him. "Why won't you believe me, after all I've done for you over the years?"

"Done for me? Is that some kind of joke? You've bled me dry most of the time. Look at us, we're living in a house mortgaged to the hilt—not my choice, I hasten to add. You sit around here all day like Lady Muck, go out for lunch with friends and to the spa for all sorts of treatments on *my* salary. And all the time... I was living with a murderer. You killed her, Gail, and lived with that knowledge for five years, never hinting at what you'd done. Jesus, you're a cold-hearted woman, and I can't believe I've stayed with you all these years. It makes me shudder, the thought of sharing that bed with you."

Dee flinched, clearly hurt by his words. She let him rant, and once he'd finished, she inhaled a breath and let out a demented laugh. "You're a loser with a capital L. You're to blame for her death. If you hadn't poked her with that dick of yours, she'd still be alive today, probably."

"What? You knew about the affair?"

Another sinister laugh left Dee's lips. "Are you for fucking real? You're an open book, Alan. I know what you're thinking before you even think it, most of the time. I used to follow you to your secret assignations with that *slut*."

"You didn't. Why didn't you say something?"

"And come down to your level when there were other ways of dealing with the problem? Dream on, man. You make me sick."

"Likewise. I'll go one better, you make my skin crawl. Every time... nope, I refuse to go there." He faced Sally and said, "Get her out of my house. I hope she gets banged up for the rest of her life."

Dee flew at Alan, managing to scratch a deep cut down the length of his cheek before Jordan and Stuart could restrain her. They removed the cursing woman from the house and placed her in the back of their car.

Alan held a hand to his face. "She's left her mark on me in more ways than one. I feel sick to the stomach, knowing what she did five years ago. Had I had an inkling about the truth, I would have reported her to the police. You have to believe me."

Sally rubbed his arm. "We do. Are you going to be all right?"

"I will be, providing you keep her locked up."

"You can guarantee it."

"Can you tell me how you knew?"

"Her accomplice dobbed her in during an interview at the

station this evening, while you were being interviewed in the other room."

"Accomplice? Who is he?"

"We've yet to get to the bottom of how they met. But she had some kind of hold over him. They got involved in a game of truth and dare, a dangerous game that resulted in two innocent people losing their lives."

He sank onto the bed and covered his face with his hands. "I didn't know her at all. They were like chalk and cheese, her and Gail, no comparison. I often wondered what I saw in her. Dee, I mean. That question will be running through my mind every day I have left in this world. What an absolute bitch."

"You will never have to see her again. She'll spend years behind bars. She won't be able to talk her way out of this one, I promise you."

"I'm glad. I hope she rots in prison."

THEY SAID farewell to Alan at the door. He appeared to be a relieved but a broken man, all the same. Sally glanced at the car behind before getting in her vehicle. Stuart was in the back of the car, which Sally believed most likely as Dee had kicked off once they'd put her in the vehicle. Dee stared at the house she had shared with Alan and shook her head.

Sally gave the thumbs-up to Jordan, and he drew away from the kerb and carried out a three-point turn. Sally did the same, and they headed back to the station.

During the journey, Sally's mobile rang. She pressed the button to answer it. "Joanna, you're on speaker. Any news for us?"

"Yes, boss. A patrol has just located Phil Thomas's car at a disused warehouse. The officers haven't approached the scene but called it in right away and are monitoring the situation at a safe distance."

"Great news. It's all coming together nicely. Give us the location. We'll shoot over there now. Let's hope he hasn't done anything rash to Steve Morton. We've just arrested Dee Armstrong for Gail's murder. If he hears about that, hopefully he'll reconsider his actions."

"Great news. Here's hoping. The warehouse is on the edge of Kimberley." Joanna went on to give the postcode which Lorne entered into the satnav.

"We'll get back to you soon. Thanks, Jo." Sally ended the call. "Will you contact Jordan, tell him to go on ahead and explain the situation to him?"

Lorne used Sally's phone as it was lying between them.

As soon as Lorne had hung up, Sally switched on the siren. They arrived at the warehouse within ten minutes and pulled up alongside the patrol car. Sally and Lorne rushed over to the two uniformed officers. One of them was observing the warehouse through binoculars. He offered them to Sally for her to take a look.

"Top window, ma'am. He's pacing the floor, seems mighty anxious to me."

"Okay, we're going to need an Armed Response Team to help us. There's no way we'll be able to get up there without him being aware of our presence. That would put the hostage at risk. I'll get on to the commander now." Sally passed the binoculars to Lorne and stepped back a few paces to make the call.

Control informed her the ART would be with them within twenty minutes.

As it was, they arrived within twelve. After Sally consulted with the commanding officer, he took charge of the situation. Sally had pleaded with him to try and negotiate with Phil first. To get the message across that they had two killers at the station being charged with his sister's murder and that Steve had nothing to do with the crime, after all.

The commanding officer did as requested. The hostage situation was brought to a swift and successful conclusion. Phil was taken away in handcuffs by the patrol officers, while Sally and Lorne ferried Steve to hospital to get checked over. After he was given the all-clear, they delivered him back home, to his children. The time by now was coming up to midnight.

Sally dropped Lorne off at home and continued on her way. Simon greeted her at the doorway with a much-needed and well-deserved glass of vintage wine from his vast collection.

"God, I'm in dire need of this." Sally took a sip of the welcome wine.

"It's been a long day for you." He wrapped an arm around her shoulders and drew her in for a kiss.

Dex bounced around at their feet, fearing he was missing out on all the attention. Sally stroked him and crouched to give him a cuddle.

"Are you hungry?" Simon asked. He headed into the kitchen and opened the oven.

The delicious aroma made her stomach rumble.

"I wasn't, but I am now. What's on the menu?"

"I made a chicken curry. I can reheat a jacket potato or put some rice on to boil, but that will mean it'll be twenty minutes before you eat."

"I'm fine with a bowl of curry and a naan bread."

Simon dished up her dinner, and they sat at the kitchen table with Dex curled up at her feet, as usual.

"So, what happened?" Simon asked after she'd bolted down a couple of mouthfuls.

"Anything and everything. To sum it all up, we have two

killers behind bars and a hostage released and safely back home with his children."

"What will happen to the brother?"

"Phil will have to be charged, but I'll have a word in his defence. He was under severe stress and thought he was doing the right thing."

"Will the CPS see it that way?"

Sally's mouth turned down. "Not sure. All I can do is try."

"You're amazing." Simon smiled lovingly.

"You're not so bad yourself. This is scrummy. I'm going to suffer, eating curry at this time of night."

"Who cares? How did Lorne get on, filling Jack's shoes?"

"It was wonderful working with her again, but don't tell Jack. He's mardy enough most days as it is, I couldn't bear it if he got any worse."

"Your secret is safe with me."

# EPILOGUE

The following day was hectic for all the team, tying up most of the loose ends. Sally had broken the news to Tania's husband, Tim, who had been shocked but also relieved to know the truth at last after five years of living with the uncertainty of knowing whether his wife was alive or not.

Dee had been interviewed a few times during the day, but Sally had received the same response from her to every question: "No comment." But there would be no doubt she would go down for both crimes with James Trout's full confession to hand. They had Dee Armstrong bang to rights, whether she realised it or not. Later that day, she was sent to the remand centre to spend the next few months behind bars before the case went to trial.

Sally had also received the confirmation from Pauline that the body in the lake was that of Gail Morton. A DNA sample from the mother had matched the bone marrow that had been removed from the victim's leg.

At five o'clock, or thereabouts, the team were getting ready to go home for a barbecue planned at Sally and

Simon's when Sally received a call from Pat Sullivan on the front desk.

"Sorry to trouble you, ma'am, but there's a young lady in reception whom I believe you should have a word with."

"Is it in relation to an ongoing case, Pat?"

"Yes, I believe so."

"Give me two minutes and I'll be down." She ended the call and entered the outer office. "So, no excuses from anyone. Simon has insisted I invite you and your partners, and any ankle biters you have at home, to our place for a celebratory barbecue tonight. Make the necessary calls home, I'm wanted at the front desk."

"Everything all right?" Lorne asked, concerned.

"I won't know until I get there. Do you want to come with me?"

"Why not? It'll save me having to tie you down later to get the news out of you."

They left the office and laughed all the way down the stairs.

Opening the door to reception, they found a distressed-looking female standing next to Pat.

"Ah, here they are now, the detectives you need to speak to. DI Parker and DS Warner, this is Christine Newman."

Sally smiled at the woman and gave the desk sergeant a quizzical look. "Am I missing something?"

"The Billy Prather case," Lorne mumbled beside her.

"No. Are you the girlfriend?" Sally asked, shocked.

The woman's legs gave way beneath her. If it hadn't been for Pat's quick reactions to save her, she would have ended up flat out on the floor. He settled her in one of the black plastic chairs along the far wall.

Pat removed his hands and stood back. "Take your time, there's no rush. Or would you rather I tell the detectives?"

Christine pulled a tissue from her small leather shoulder

bag, dried her tears and then wiped her nose. "Would you? I find it so traumatic to tell the story over and over."

"Of course. Yes, DS Warner, you were right. This young lady is the girlfriend of Billy Prather. At the time she went missing, she had amnesia and was unable to come forward to inform us that she was still alive."

"I'm so sorry to hear that, Christine. Can I ask why your family didn't tell the police on your behalf?" Sally asked.

"Because my mother detested Billy. She couldn't wait to get me out of his clutches." Christine paused to refill her lungs. "She sent me to Devon, to live with her sister. It wasn't until Mum died of cancer that the truth came out. Then, bit by bit, things started to make sense and my memory returned."

"How traumatic for you, and that's why you're here today, to tell the truth?"

"Yes. I did some research on the internet and found out that Billy was serving a long sentence for killing *me*. You have to let him go. As you can see, I'm not dead and I never have been. Please, won't you help me?"

"Without a doubt. Thank you for coming forward, although we'll need to carry out some background checks first to make sure you are who you say you are. Do you have any ID on you?"

"Yes, my driving licence and my birth certificate. I found them in my mother's belongings after the funeral. I have been living under a different name with my aunt for the past five years."

Sally shook her head in disbelief. "I'm sorry your family put you through such an ordeal. Are you fully recovered now, or are things still sketchy?"

"I know enough to recognise that I still love Billy and want to do my very best to help set him free."

"So do I," Sally agreed. "It might not be possible to get the ball rolling this evening, but you have my word that I will be on the phone to several departments first thing in the morning."

"Thank you. It means the world to me that you're prepared to believe me."

"I'll leave you in Sergeant Sullivan's capable hands. Give him your contact number, and I'll get back to you soon, hopefully with some good news."

"I can't thank you enough. Will it take long to get him released?"

"I'll do my best to ensure it happens swiftly. Bear with me, okay? It could take weeks, there again, it might take a matter of days, who knows? But I won't let it drop until he's out. Go home, get some rest, I'll call you soon."

The young woman wiped her eyes on a fresh tissue, and Pat sat next to her, his notebook in hand, ready to take down her details.

On the way back upstairs, Sally said, "Carol was right, again."

Lorne nodded. "I tell you, it's not often she's wrong, and on the odd occasion she is, she gets so frustrated with herself."

THE BARBECUE WAS A HUGE SUCCESS. Everyone chipped in, either by stopping off at the off-licence or the supermarket on the way and picking up bottles of wine and lager, or helping to prepare the salad and carry the food outside. Twenty people to cater for, all starving after a hard day's shift.

"Are you all right about this, Simon?" Sally asked.

"Hey, this is great. You guys all deserve to be treated to a good dinner and excellent company after what you've been through. What's that?"

"It sounded like the bell." Sally frowned. "I thought everyone was here. I'll go, it's probably a delivery or something."

"I'll flip the steaks over."

Sally just caught the twinkle in his eye as he turned away. *Hmm... what are you up to?* She wound her way through the crowd and into the house, accompanied by Dex. "Who can this be, boy?"

Dex bounced up and down on the spot and wagged his tail.

Sally opened the door and gasped. "What the...? Heck, I wasn't expecting you. Come in, here, give me your bag. Your mother is going to have a heart attack when you walk out there." She hugged her visitor and took her overnight bag from her, then led her out into the garden. "Stay behind me."

"She's going to see me, I'm taller than you, Sally."

"Don't rub it in. You'll just have to duck down. Dex, stop pestering her." Sally made her way back through the crowd, her gaze seeking out Simon, who gave her a knowing wink. She reached her destination and tapped Lorne on the shoulder.

"This is great, Sally. Give me a shout if you need me to ferry anything else out of the house."

"I have a surprise for you." Sally took a couple of steps to the side to reveal Charlie.

"What the...? Charlie! What are you doing here?" Lorne asked, finally finding her voice.

"Blame Carol. She made me feel guilty for not seeing you more often. I managed to wangle a few days leave and here I am."

Lorne and Tony hugged their daughter.

"We've missed you," Lorne said, tears emerging.

And before long, Carol joined in the group hug.

Sally walked away from the touching scene and sought out her husband. "You knew about this and didn't tell me?"

"Some secrets aren't meant to be shared, for the good of others."

"I love you, you're the best husband ever to have walked this earth."

He wrapped his arms around her and pulled her close. "And you're the best wife a man could ever wish for."

They raised a glass, and Sally said, "To us. To our friends and family." She glanced around the crowd at the people who enriched her life daily at work and at home. Proud to have every single one of them by her side.


THE END



THANK you for reading Truth or Dare, Sally and Lorne will return in a few months with another thrilling cold case or two.


IN THE MEANTIME, have you read any of my fast paced other crime thrillers yet? Why not try the first book in the DI Sara Ramsey series No Right to Kill


OR GRAB the first book in the bestselling, award-winning, Justice series here, Cruel Justice.


OR THE FIRST book in the spin-off Justice Again series, Gone In Seconds.

. . .

Why not try the first book in the DI Sam Cobbs series, set in the beautiful Lake District, To Die For.

Perhaps you'd prefer to try one of my other police procedural series, the DI Kayli Bright series which begins with The Missing Children.

Or maybe you'd enjoy the DI Sally Parker series set in Norfolk, Wrong Place.

Or my gritty police procedural starring DI Nelson set in Manchester, Torn Apart.

Or maybe you'd like to try one of my successful psychological thrillers She's Gone, I KNOW THE TRUTH or Shattered Lives.

# KEEP IN TOUCH WITH M A COMLEY

Pick up a FREE novella by signing up to my newsletter today.
https://BookHip.com/WBRTGW

BookBub
**www.bookbub.com/authors/m-a-comley**

Blog

http://melcomley.blogspot.com

Why not join my special Facebook group to take part in monthly giveaways.

Readers' Group

Printed in Great Britain
by Amazon